The Streets Don't Love Nobody

By Tranay Adams

I0587609

The Streets Don't Love Nobody

Copyright © 2018 Tranay Adams. All rights reserved.

Warning: The unauthorized reproduction or distribution of this work is illegal. Criminal copyright infringement, including infringement without monetary gain, is investigated by FBI and is punishable by up to five (5) years in federal prison and a fine of $250,000.

All names, characters, and incidents depicted in this book are products of the author's imagination or are used fictitiously. Any resemblance to actual events, locales, organizations, or persons, living or dead, is entirely coincidental, and beyond the intent of the author and publisher.

No part of this book may be reproduced or transmitted in any form or by any means, electronic or mechanical, including photocopying, recording, or by any information storage and retrieval system, without permission in writing from the publisher.

The Streets Don't Love Nobody/ Tranay Adams-1st ed. © 2018

Editor: The Ghost

Cover Artist: Designrans

Publisher: Tranay Adams

The Streets Don't Love Nobody

Chapter One

Buzzzzzzz!

The huge iron door of the federal correctional facility rolled back. Shortly thereafter, a hulk of a man strolled out. He had a big bald head, and the lower half of his face was covered in salt and pepper stubble. The muscular man smiled from ear to ear and took in his surroundings. At that moment, he realized that freedom was something that the average person took for granted, and he vowed then that he'd never be one of those persons again.

Big Meat had butterflies in his stomach the closer his release date came. He didn't know what to expect with it having been ten years since he'd been from behind the walls. If he was asked to describe the feeling, he'd have to say it was the equivalent of him getting his first brick of coke, or his first time getting some pussy. He remembered both of those events like they were yesterday, and he'd never forget them.

Big Meat made his way down the sidewalk until he came upon a Chevron gas station that doubled as a convenience store. He dipped inside of the store and got himself a 35 cent bag of Fritos and a Sprite, to bust the fifty dollar bill he had on him to use at one of the only working telephone booths in the area. As soon as Big Meat purchased his items, he pushed his way out of the store's glass door and walked to the booth out on the sidewalk. He searched the tattered Pacific Bell telephone book for a listing for nearby cab companies until he found one closest to him. He found himself waiting twenty minutes before a yellow taxi cab pulled up. After discarding his empty bag of chips and beverage bottle, he brushed the crumbs from off his palms and hopped into the back seat of the cab.

The Streets Don't Love Nobody

***

As soon as the cab stopped, Big Meat hit the driver with the bread for the fare and hopped out. A smile stretched across his face as he approached Tam's burgers, which was a famous ghetto burger joint. He rubbed his hands together hungrily as he feasted his eyes on the menu. His eyes were as big as his stomach, and he'd been dreaming about that double bacon cheese burger and fries for the past week. He told himself that as soon as he was released from The Beast he was going to get a number 4#.

Big Meat had spent a great portion of his money on the cab he'd caught to Tam's, but he felt like it was well worth it. He'd been eating prison food for the entire ten years he'd been incarcerated, and he couldn't wait to get his hands on the food on the outside. Although he'd have to catch the bus to his grandmother's house after eating, he wasn't tripping off of it. The way he saw it, at least he'd be satisfied with his first meal.

"My man," Big Meat began, massaging his chin as he studied the menu above his head. "Lemmie getta number 4# with bacon, and swap that medium soda out with a chocolate shake."

Big Meat dug into his pocket as he watched the Mexican man jot down his order on a small notepad. The Mexican man told him how much his food would cost and tore off his ticket number, handing it to him. Big Meat passed him the money for his meal and waited for his change. Once he'd paid for his food, he sat down at the table, watching the cars driving back and forth across his line of vision. Before Big Meat knew it, the Mexican dude that had taken his order, called him forth to get his food. The big man retrieved the bag and bid homeboy farewell. He indulged in his chocolate shake as he made his way towards the bus stop bench. He sat down on the bench and pulled out his burger, removing the yellow wrapper. The first bite brought a great, big smile to his face, eyelids shut.

Hearing someone approaching from his right, Big Meat looked to find a rather skinny, bearded dude in a wheelchair. The man wore black sunglasses and his hair in five cornrows which were slightly frizzy. He was dressed in a plaid red flannel and Dickies. A thick wool blanket lie over his lap, and his red All Star Chuck Taylors with the fat laces peeked from underneath it

Big Meat eyeballed the man curiously, wondering how he'd landed himself in that wheelchair for the rest of his life. He knew it was in bad taste for him to stare, but he found himself unable to look away. Homeboy in the wheelchair didn't pay Big Meat any mind, as he whipped his wheelchair around and sat it down so he'd be facing the street. He pulled a pack of Newport 100's from out of the top pocket of his flannel and flipped open the lid of it. He pulled one of the cigarettes out with his lips. Afterwards, he fished a Bic lighter from out of his pocket and put fire to the end of his square. Sucking on the end of the Joe caused the tip of it to glow ember. He blew smoke from out of his nostrils and mouth, watching the traffic in front of his eyes.

During this entire time, Big Meat kept his eyes glued on this man, jaws swollen with the cheese burger he'd been munching on.

"Go on and take a picture, homie, it'll last longer." Homeboy in the wheelchair said, staring straight ahead, blowing smoke into the air.

The fact that dude in the wheelchair knew he was staring at him without turning his head startled Big Meat.

2

The Streets Don't Love Nobody

"My bad, homie," Big Meat apologized and turned his attention back to the streets. He went back to eating his cheese burger and enjoying his shake.

"It's all good, OG." Homeboy told him, looking at him for the first time, wafting cigarette pinched between his fingers. "What's yo' name?"

Big Meat munched the last of the food down in his mouth. He then turned to the nigga in the wheelchair, and said, "Meat…Big Meat."

"I'm Dirty Redd, my nigga." homeboy in the wheelchair leaned to his left and dapped up Big Meat.

"'Sup, Redd?" Big Meat said, and then went back to eating.

"Ain't shit," he responded. "You fresh out, huh?"

Big Meat shot a frown at Dirty Redd. He couldn't believe he knew he'd just gotten out of federal lockup. "Yeah, I just came home. How'd you know?"

"I been on lock a couple of times, G. You got that look."

"Oh, yeah? What look is that?"

He shrugged and said, "Hard to explain, but chu wearing the same look as me when I first left from behind them walls."

Big Meat nodded his understanding and focused his attention back on his burger.

"You mind me asking what chu was locked up for?" Dirty Redd asked him.

"You see, I got what chu call a don't ask don't tell policy."

Dirty Redd nodded, feeling where Big Meat was coming from. He was all up in his business, so he expected that response.

"I feel you, my nigga, but chu can't blame a nigga for being curious. I mean, shit, you were curious, too. I seen you eyeballing my chair when I was rolling up over here," he patted his chair lovingly. You would have thought it was his girl or some shit. "I could tell you wanted to know how I got in this mothafucka, right? Don't front." He angled his head grinning, and looking at him like, *Come on now, keep it real.*

"Yeah, you got me there. I was wondering how you winded up in that bitch."

"Well, lemmie be the first to tell you, I for damn sho' ain't no Vietnam war veteran." he assured him with a smile as he blew smoke out of the corner of his mouth. What he had said got Big Meat grinning, too. "I tell you what. I'ma tell you how I ended up paralyzed and in this chair, but only if you tell me what chu did to wind up incarcerated. We gotta deal?" he extended his fist towards Big Meat.

Big Meat looked at Dirty Redd's fist for a while, allowing it to linger in the air. He brushed the crumbs from off his hand and made a fist, outstretching it towards Dirty Redd. They touched fists and made the deal.

"Alright," Dirty Redd began with a deep breath, about to tell his story.

***

The Streets Don't Love Nobody

The sun was beaming its brightest with its rays deflecting off everything in the neighborhood. The birds were chirping, children were laughing and playing, dogs were barking and the sound of gunfire had rung out. Shortly thereafter, an ambulance siren and police sirens could be heard far off in the distance. It was safe to say that it was the average day in the hood.

Just then, the sound of George Clinton's *Atomic Dog* grew closer and closer on the corner of Adams and Griffith, as it was approaching hastily. The noise of screeching tires filled the air and at that precise moment, a sexy ass cherry red '64 Chevy Impala made a sharp turn at the end of the block, on three wheels. Its gold trimmings and fourteen inch Dayton rims shining beneath the rays of the sun. All that could be seen inside of the old school whip were two heads. One was wearing a red bandana around his head, Tupac style, and was position behind the wheel. While the other wore a Cardinals fitted cap high up and cocked to the side on his head. He was sitting on the passenger side and holding the outside frame of the door, as the Chevy bent the corner in a hurry and threatened to spill him over into the driver's seat beside his homeboy.

Why must I feel like that

Why must I chase the cat

Nothin' but the dog in me

Do the dogcatcher, dogcatcher

Do the dogcatcher

Do the dogcatcher, dogcatcher

Do the dogcatcher

"Nigga, you gon' flip this mothafucka over, slow this bitch down!" Menace complained to his right-hand man, Flocka, creases in his forehead. He was a brown-skinned dude standing five- foot-ten in height and weighing in around 170 lbs. A toothpick was at the corner of his mouth, wagging up and down every time he talked. He filled out a black T-shirt, black Dickies and red All Star Converses. A gold necklace hung around his neck and was attached to his name plate which was in Old English letters: Menace. A plain faced, gold Rolex adorned his wrist. It was simple, but matched perfectly with his necklace.

Menace had practically raised himself due to his mother's death and his father being strung out on dope. He took to the streets early as fuck. He started out holding the guns and drugs for the trap stars around his way. From there, he went to lookout, to slinging crack himself. That was until Big Meat brought him into his organization. Once Big Meat had put him down, he put Flocka down. Now the homies were getting money together.

"Fallback, Blood, I got this." Flocka cracked a smile, showcasing his top row of shiny gold teeth. He favored the late great Tupac Shakur, especially with the diamond nose piercing, long eye lashes, thick eyebrows and mustache. His red bandana matched right along with his throwback Jordan 23 jersey. He had two Jesus head medallion necklaces around his neck; one of which was a size smaller than the other. The Rolex he had on was a little bit flashier than his homeboy's though. Plus, he had an icy gold ring on every finger of both hands.

Flocka's parents were high school sweethearts; crazy in love psychopaths that harbored a taste for blood and carnage. The psychotic mothafuckaz went on one of the most

6

talked about robbing and killing sprees on the west coast, taking an infant Flocka along for the ride. The deranged couple eventually met their end when they were cornered by police at a seedy motel out in Austin, Texas. The killaz had a two hour shootout with the law until they were fatally wounded. Flocka, who was still a baby then, was bounced around through the system, until he was eleven-years-old. He ran away from foster care and into the welcoming arms of the streets, where he survived by robbing, stealing, and selling crack. He met Menace by chance when he was just thirteen-years-old. The young thug had saved Flocka's life. He beat a hustler with a baseball bat that was going to blow Flocka's brains out for cheating him in a crap game, with a pair of loaded dice. Ever since then, the two of them had been down for each other, like they had been pushed out of the same womb.

The '64 came down on all four tires and sped off down the residential street. Its owner hit the switches on it and made it jump up and down, straight up stunting. Some of everyone out on the streets that day face lit up and they pointed at the flashy car, telling whomever was beside them how hard it looked.

Flocka narrowed his eyes and peered closer through the windshield. "Yo', ain't that lil' momma that lives next door to you? What's her name? Shanea or some shit?" he took a quick glance at Menace.

"Shatira," he corrected him as he chuckled and shook his head.

"Yeah, that's right, Shatira. Baby is stacked like a mothafucka, boyyy. Goddddamn!" he made an ugly face seeing Shatira walk up the block beside her friend, switching from left to right. Her ass looked like she was concealing two basketballs inside of her black Capri pants. She was in a white baby T-shirt with Princess emblazoned across it. Her enormous breasts made the *Princess* look like it was 3D. Her long wavy hair was pulled back in a bun and a Chinese bang hung over her forehead, giving shade to her almond shaped eyes. Her rich chocolate skin was damn near flawless, save for a few acne scars she'd gotten from puberty. "Yo', you hittin' that yet, my nigga?"

"Gone, man," Menace looked away smiling, dimples dominant in his cheeks. The truth was he was feeling Shatira, but he had yet to step to her. He flirted with her here and there but that was it.

"Aww, man, I can't believe you. She stay next door, you 'pose to be wearin' that ass out. Especially with all of this paper we gettin'. Shiiiit, name a bitch out here that ain't tryna fuck with us. You feel me?"

"Yeah, I feel you."

Flocka nodded to the windshield at old girl that was walking next to Shatira, which prompted Menace to look. She was in a wife beater and Daisy Dukes, with the pockets hanging out of the bottoms of them. She had on a pair of blue Chuck Taylors without socks. "Who is that with her?"

"Her homegirl, Cee Cee," Menace answered him, staring through the windshield at Shatira's friend now. She had a walnut complexion and her hair was braided into pig tails on either side. There had Bamboo earrings in her lobes that spelled out her name, *Cee Cee*, and a diamond nose stud in her right nostril. Baby girl had a ghetto sex appeal that had niggaz checking for her all day every day.

"That lil' bitch bad, too."

8

The Streets Don't Love Nobody

"Oh, fa sho'."

"I'm tryna fuck that lil' bitch Cee Cee, I'ma pull up." Flocka mashed the gas pedal and his hood classic ripped up the street, sitting high up off the ground on its four rims.

***

"Girl, it's hot as a bitch out here." Cee Cee said, wiping her shiny forehead with the back of her hand and then fanning her face. "I wish the sun would give a bitch a break."

Cee Cee was a military brat. Her family moved from Florida, to Connecticut, to Nebraska, before finally settling in Los Angeles, where she attended Jefferson high school. Cee Cee's father wanted his daughter to know how to defend herself so he taught her how to box and properly fire a variety of firearms. The girl could handle herself quite well, so a lot of chicks didn't fuck with her.

"Who you telling? I'm thirsty as a mug, shoot. I can't wait to get up in this house to get me something to drink." Shatira used the end of her shirt to wipe off her glistening face.

"Yo', what's up with ol' boy I saw yo' next door neighbor talking to the other day?"

"Who?" she frowned, curious as to whom her homegirl was talking about.

"Homeboy with all of jewels on and shit, he was pushing an all red old school. A low rider, I think."

"Oh, I think that's his friend Flocka."

"Well, Flocka is fiiine, and he looks like he's paid from what I see. Now, I normally don't fuck with niggaz unless they pushing something that's around this year, but he'll get a pass since his ass is so fine." She said as she looked over her French Tip manicured nails.

"Ooooh, yo' hoe ass is conceited, bitch, how you know he won't chu?" Shatira smirked.

"Bitch, be serious, who don't won't me?" Cee Cee curled her finger up in one of her pigtails, "Niggaz stay checking for a bitch but they don't get the time of day 'less they willing to pay to play, ya feel me?" she chuckled and held out her fist for dap.

Shatira dapped her right-hand girl up and said, "I feel you, but I don't get down like that. See, I'm saving myself for my one and only." she batted her eyelashes and a big, beautiful smile spread across her face, showcasing her pearly white teeth. Although she was only seventeen- years-old, she saw herself being with one man and one man only, for the rest of her life. She wasn't going to be out there in the streets like a lot of girls she knew, busting it wide open for dope boys, just because they was pushing something fly and playing with a couple of dollars. Nah, she wanted to meet someone, date, fall in love, get married and have children. You know, the old fashion way, like the older folks?

"I ain't mad at cha, sis. We all gotta dream, and ain't nothing wrong with that."

Hearing George Clinton's *Atomic Dog*, the girls heads whipped around and they found Flocka's old school Chevy speeding down the street. The throwback vehicle came to a halt beside them alongside the curb. Seeing Shatira from the passenger side, Menace threw his head back at her like,

The Streets Don't Love Nobody

What's up? And she blushed and smiled, looking away, shyly. Right after, Menace and Flocka hopped out of the '64, approaching the ladies, confidently. Cee Cee eyed Flocka seductively and twisted her French Tip nail at the corner of her teeth, enticing him. He shot her a sexy ass grin and threw his head back, pulling his sagging Levi's upon his waistline.

"Yo', Tira, come here for a minute!" Menace motioned for Shatira to come to him as he advanced in her direction, smiling. You could tell that they were feeling one another on some level, because they were both smiling as hard as they ever had when they saw each other. Although Shatira tried her best to hide it, she was self conscious whenever she was around the young gangsta. She stood still while trying to figure out whether she should go over to him or continue on her way home. As she was trying to make up her mind, Cee Cee nudged her in Menace's direction, making up her mind for her.

"What's up?" she blushed harder, looking down at her feet and then back up at Menace. She then hoisted the brown paper bag up under her arm, trying to get a good hold of it.

Standing in front of Menace and Flocka, Shatira could tell that they were getting money by their attire and how they carried themselves. They were fresh to death and their jewels were icy. In fact, their jewels were so icy that she and Cee Cee had to squint their eyes from the sunlight deflecting off of them creating blinding glares.

"What's up with chu, slim? Where you running off to?" Menace asked.

"I just left my homegirl's house; I'm headed to my crib now." Shatira said.

"Oh, okay, I was going to see if you wanted to hang out with me for a while, but I see that chu busy. How about this? You take my number down and we can get up once you have some free time."

Shatira didn't know what to say because she had always had a crush on Menace, but she never thought that he would show any interest in her. She turned to see what Cee Cee thought, but she was in her own world, getting acquainted with Menace's boy, Flocka. Menace noticed that Shatira seemed unsure so he grabbed her hand and walked her away from the group so that they could be alone.

"'Sup, ma? You seem a lil' nervous." he cracked a sexy grin and licked his lips, massaging the shallow goatee that outlined his mouth.

"Umm, I'm not that nervous." She looked away shyly, her chocolate cheeks turning red.

"Okay, well, look, I'm not tryna hold you up. I know you probably got shit to do, so how about you take down my number and we'll chop it up whenever you get a minute."

"Actually, I don't have a cell right now."

Menace was shocked that someone her age wouldn't have a cell phone of her own. He reached into his pocket and handed her one of the IPhones that he had in his pocket. He had one cell phone for street business and one for personal use. He let little momma hold his personal joint. He wasn't fucking with any other chicks then, so he wasn't worried about anyone hitting him up on it. Besides, any of his homies or family that hit him up on his personal cellular would hit his business phone. That was if it was really important. Niggas knew better than to be banging his business line if it wasn't life or death.

"Here take this. You can have this phone, and don't worry about paying the bill. I got it faded."

"Okay. Thanks, Jeremy." She smiled, sliding the cellular into his back pocket.

Menace's forehead wrinkled and he gave her the side eye. "Jeremy? You calling outta nigga's government and shit."

"Oops, my bad, it's Menace now, right?" she smiled harder.

"Yep. That's what the streets calling my boy." Flocka interjected, coming from out of nowhere and throwing his arm around his homeboy's shoulders. He was holding his cellular phone in his other hand. He was in the middle of programming Cee Cee's number into it before he threw himself into Shatira and Menace's conversation. "He damn sure earned it. My ace done put in crazy work."

"Chill, my nigga," Menace gave him a stern look and a little nudge. He didn't want him putting his business out there in the streets. What he had done in the concrete jungle was between him and whoever he had done it with.

"My bad, bruh," Flocka said. He then turned to Cee Cee. "Yo', slim, what's the last numbers of yo' math?" he finished punching in the digits that she'd given him and stashed his cellular inside of his pocket. "Alright, I'ma holla, maybe we can get together and paint the town red. You feel me?"

"That's what's up." Cee Cee smiled, her thumb caressing Flocka's Jesus head medallion as she held it in her manicured hand. Her thirsty ass couldn't help wondering how much it cost and how much the young nigga was holding.

"All right then, show a brother some love." Flocka held open his arms and she threw her arms around him, staring into his eyes lovingly. To Shatira and Menace's surprise, she kissed Flocka hard, deep and lustfully, as he cupped her bodacious ass. When they pulled away, she wiped the corners of her mouth having gotten some of his saliva around her lips. He wiped his lips with the back of his jeweled hand and eyed her hungrily, smacking her on her ample bottom as she walked over to stand on the sidewalk and wait on Shatira.

"Well, I guess I'll talk to you later. Bye." Shatira waved goodbye to Menace.

"All right, later," Menace threw up the duces. He then started to head back to the Chevy beside Flocka.

Shatira and Cee Cee went on about their business, passing up children that were in the streets playing around. A few of them looked alive when they saw the young men headed back to the Chevy Impala.

"Aye, that's Menace and Flocka!" one of the ghetto children called out to the others.

"That ain't them, stupid!" another one of the ghetto children responded.

"Wait, that is them!" a third child said, confirming it.

"Aye, hey, hey, yo'!" the children called out different things.

The children came together and waved at them. They loved Flocka and Menace because anytime that they'd see them they'd give them money and/or buy them something off the ice cream truck.

Flocka and Menace turned around. Seeing that he had the children's undivided attention, and that this was the perfect time for him to stunt in front of Cee Cee, Flocka pulled out a wad of money and removed the rubber band on it that held it together.

"Y'all lil' niggaz come here, so I can spread the wealth. Y'all come here." Flocka waved the ghetto children over and they took off running in his direction, swarming him and his right-hand man like lotuses.

Cee Cee stopped down the block and waved at Flocka, smiling. He threw his head back and gifted her with a smile before passing out some money to the kids surrounding him.

Yeah, that nigga getting to the money, and once I put this pussy on him, he gone be as sprung as a chicken. Cluck! Cluck! Cluck! Hahahahaha, Cee Cee laughed to herself and continued on down the block beside her sister from another mister.

Once Flocka was done stunting and fronting, he and Menace hopped back inside of the Impala. As soon as Flocka cranked his big boy toy up, he took off down the block, hitting switches in the old school Chevy.

"Where we off to now?" Menace inquired. His hand was resting on the window pane and the wind that was rushing inside of the car was ruffling his clothing.

"Where we were supposed to have been going before we got caught up with them broads." Flocka answered as he turned the volume up on the George Clinton song.

Tranay Adams

Chapter Two

Shatira dapped up Cee Cee and they went their separate ways. Shatira headed up the steps of her house and fished around inside of her pocket, grabbing her keys. She slid the copper key into the dead bolt and turned it, unlocking it. She then pushed open the door. As soon as she crossed the threshold, she was overwhelmed by the sound of Madden coming from the large flat-screen TV. Her stepbrothers, LaRon and Levon, sat before the television. Their tongues hung from the side of their mouths as their controllers rocked from left to right. This was due to their pressing the buttons while their eyes focused on the tube.

LaRon and Levon were Delores's identical twin sons. They were both pale skinned African Americans with freckles on their faces and auburn hair. The only difference between them was Levon's hair was in cornrows and he had a barely visible goatee. His younger brother on the other hand, LaRon, hair was in a small tapered afro. As soon as Shatira laid her eyes on them, she rolled her pupils and shut the door. Once the door clicked shut, the twins' eyes were on her. The oldest of them paused their game. LaRon licked his lips while Levon bit down on his bottom lip and grabbed the bulge in his sweatpants.

"'Sup, lil' momma?" Levon greeted his stepsister, molesting her with his eyes.

"Yeah, sup, lil' momma?" LaRon said after his brother.

"Nothing much." She said nonchalantly as she journeyed inside of the kitchen and grabbed a cup down from the cupboard. She then opened the refrigerator and leaned down. She searched through the top shelf until he found what

17

she was looking for, a carton of fruit punch Minute Made. After pouring up a cup of juice, she sat the carton of juice back inside of the refrigerator and shut it. Next, she opened the freezer and grabbed a couple of ice cubes, dropping them inside of her cup.

Shatira went to take a drink from her cup, when the freezer's door was pushed shut, startling her. With furrowed brows, she looked to her right and found Levon. He licked his lips and bit down on his bottom one, as he eyed her hungrily.

"'Sup, lil' momma?" Levon repeated, groping the bulge in his sweatpants. When she saw this, it made her cringe and she looked disgusted. She took another sip of her drink and rolled her eyes.

Taking an annoyed breath, Shatira responded, "Hey. Excuse me." she went to walk out of the kitchen and Levon slid into her path. She placed her hand on her hip and looked at him like, *I'm not in the mood, nigga.*

"Where you goin', boo?" Levon approached her, placing his hands on her waist.

Swhack!

"Nigga, don't you ever put cho hands on me without permission? Fuck wrong witchu?" Shatira's eyebrows slanted and she twisted her lips up. She moved her head with attitude like all hood chicks do when they're pissed off.

"Hahahahahahahahaha!" LaRon doubled over laughing with his arms folded across his stomach.

"Bitch, what the fuck is wrong witchu?" Levon frowned.

"Nigga, it ain't even that kind of party. I don't know what kind of females you fuck with, but they ain't this."

"Ho, you been lampin' up in here for a minute now. You ain't been kickin' in moms a goddamn thang. It's time you pay what chu owe. Ass or cash! Ain't shit up in this mothafucka free!"

Shatira looked at Levon like he was crazy and said, "Whatever, nigga, I ain't got time for this! Move up out my way so I can go to my room.."

"Ass it is then," Levon began to unbuckle his belt and unzip his Dickies. "LaRon, hold this bitch down."

"I got chu faded, bro." LaRon moved to come around his brother, so he could hold Shatira down and his sibling could have his way with her.

"Aww, hell naw, y'all niggaz not 'bouta rape me!" Shatira threw the cup of juice at Levon's face and its contents splashed everywhere. Swiftly, she drew a butcher's knife from out of the wooden block on the counter.

Snikttt!

She took up her defense, moving her butcher's knife from left to right and daring the twins to come at her.

"Come on, come on, mothafuckaz! You gotta bring ass to get some! Whose gonna be the first to die!" her scowling face looked for any buyers of the wolf tickets she had for sale.

A very pissed off Levon wiped the juice from out of his face with both hands. As a result from the contents of the cup hitting him he had a red stain on his wife beater. Glaring at Shatira, Levon squared his jaws and clenched his fists, showcasing his muscular arms and vein riddled body.

"You gone pulla knife out on us, in our own house?" LaRon's forehead creased and wrinkles formed around his nose.

"Our house? You niggaz is thirty-two years old, still living witcho momma! This her punk ass house! Matter of fact, it's mine, 'cause I know she bought it with my daddy's life insurance policy funds!"

"Watch cho mouth now, you gettin' outta hand!" Levon warned as he pointed a crooked finger at her.

"No, nigga, you watch your mouth! Now, back that ass up, 'fore I carve y'all asses up like a Christmas turkey!" she brought the butcher's knife toward them and they threw up their hands, walking backwards.

"You gon' be one sorry bitch." LaRon promised.

"Not as sorry as you're gonna be should either one of y'all try me again!"

"Oh, this ain't over, we gon'…"

Smack!

Levon's head snapped to the right when Shatira had went cross his face. A red hand impression was left behind on his cheek and the side of his face was stinging and throbbing.

"Shut cho bitch ass up!" Shatira mad dogged him and bit down on the corner of her lip angrily. A vein in her neck throbbed, hatefully.

The Streets Don't Love Nobody

When Levon slowly brought his head back around, he was smiling and licking his bloody lip.

"Oh, yeeeaaah, I like it rough, baby, we gon' definitely finish this lil' game later."

"The Game of Death!" She slowly made her way around the twins and slowly backed away, going towards the living room.

"It's a date." Levon kissed his palm and blew her a kiss.

Shatira lowered her butcher's knife down at her side and headed toward her bed room, hurriedly. When she slammed the door shut behind her, the sound echoed out into the living room.

Once Shatira was gone, LaRon and Levon emerged from the kitchen looking around. When they didn't see her they lowered their guards and went back to their game of Madden.

"I'ma fuck that lil' bitch if it's the last thang I do, bro. That's on everything," Levon took the time to fire up a half smoken blunt he had earlier that day.

"Mannnn, that lil' broad ain't gon' give you no ass." LaRon made a funny face and waved him off.

Levon threw his head back and blew a cloud of smoke into the air. Bringing his head back down, he licked his lips and un-paused the game. "Oh, she gon' gemmie that ass, or I'ma take it. Straight up."

***

Tranay Adams

Shatira slammed the door shut behind her and placed her back up against the door. She sighed and wiped her forehead with the back her hand. The confrontation between her and her stepbrothers had been a close call. She thought that they were going to drive her to have to cut one of them. Although she didn't want it to have to come to that, she wasn't above killing anyone to stop them from violating her. She'd sit down for the rest of her days before she allowed any one of those perverted ass niggaz to run up in her.

Man, I'm getting tire of having to deal with these two thirsty-ass niggaz. I'ma mess around and have to kill one of them fools. I'll be glad when I turn eighteen so I can inherit that money my daddy left me. Once I get that, I'm out of here. Killa Cali ain't gon' ever see a bitch again, for real, for real.

Shatira turned around and locked her bedroom door. She then plopped down on her bed and picked up the portrait on her nightstand, leaving her butcher's knife in place of it. Behind the portrait's glass was a photo of a younger her, her father and her mother. A smile spread across Shatira's lips and tears came to her eyes. Before she knew it, her teardrops were pelting the portraits glass and sliding down it.

"Damn, daddy, I miss you so much. I wish you were here."Shatira wiped her dripping eye with her curled finger and sniffled.

Vroooooom!

A forest green Jeep Grand Cherokee ripped up the vacant rode with its bright headlights leading the way. Marion, a big bald, dark caramel complexioned man, with a bushy beard, sat behind the wheel. He and his wife, Delores, were on their way back from his parents' anniversary party out in Montgomery, Alabama.

22

The Streets Don't Love Nobody

"Honey, your baby girl hates my guts. She looks at me like I'm wearing a pointy hat and drive a goddamn broom," Delores complained about Marion's sixteen-year-old daughter, Shatira. See, Delores's best friend, Golden, was Marion's first wife and Shatira's biological mother. She'd died in a drive-by shooting two years prior. Delores and Marion ended up hooking up a year later, which was frowned upon by their friends and family, but they couldn't help that they loved one another. They tried to deny their feelings but their hearts wanted what their hearts wanted, so they gave in to their emotions. They winded up dating for a while and had gotten married two years later.

"Oh, come on, Dee, you're over exaggerating, baby girl doesn't hate your guts. She's just gotta get accustomed to this relationship. I mean, think about it, lady bug. Her mom's best friend and her father are married. That's gotta be awkward for her."

"My boys took it okay." She countered.

Marian frowned up when she said this and looked over at her. *"Shit, them two niggaz better had. Ain't them mothafuckaz thirty-one or some shit? I wish I did hear about one of them niggaz pissing and moaning about chu tying the knot."* He frowned up thinking about LaRon and Levon, his wife's kids. They were old as a mothafucka, still living with her and off her. It tripped him out that she didn't seem to mind either. On more than one occasion Delores mentioned them moving with them once they closed escrow on their new house. Although Marion hadn't said anything then, he planned on nipping that idea in the bud once she brought it up again.

Delores's face twisted up and she took a deep breath, folding her arms across her chest. Seeing this made Marion feel guilty about how his daughter was acting toward her.

23

Taking a deep breath, he took her hand and interlocked it with his. Looking back and forth between her and the windshield, he started speaking again.

"Listen, I'm gonna have a long talk with Shatira as soon as we get back home. I'm gonna lay all the cards out on the table and explain things to her. Trust me, everything is gonna be alright. I promise." Quickly, he gave her a kiss on the lips and settled back down in his seat. When he did this, he saw Delores's slightly blushing and smiling, as she tried to contain her emotions. "There we go, lemmie see that smile I love so much."

"No." she tried to hide her smiling.

"Awww, come on, let big daddy see that beautiful smile." A smile stretched across Marian's face. Constanttly looking back and forth between Delores and the windshield, he noticed that her face started give to the smile he was encouraging her to show him until it was visible. "There it go, now give big daddy some lip."

Delores unbuckled her safety belt and leaned forward. She held the side of Marion's face as she kissed him long, deep and passionately. He became so engrossed in the kiss that he forgot to keep his eyes on the road. By the time he turned around, he found a dear standing before him. The animal was frozen stiff and caught in his headlight. The bright white orbs of the SUV overwhelmed the creature and left it transfixed.

"Oh, shiiiit!" Marion's eyes bulged and his jaw dropped. He gripped the steering wheel tighter and mashed the brake pedal to the floor. Seeing that his truck was still about to collide with the deer, he whipped the steering wheel to the left. The SUV flipped over several times and spilled

wreckage out on the road. It went tumbling down the side of the road and then down a hill. Finally, stopping as it landed upside down on the ground. Its headlight still shined brightly, but smoke wafted from underneath its bent up hood.

"Uhhhhh!" Marion moaned as he hung upside down in his seat; still buckled up to his safety belt. He was bleeding at the side of his head. His nose was broken and bleeding and so was his jaw. His eyes were rolled so far to the back of his head that you could barely see their pupils. Suddenly, he began to regain focus. He looked to Delores and saw that she was dizzy. Her only injury was on her forehead. There was a nasty gash there that bled around the shape of her nose. "Dee! Dee, baby are you, okay? Are you all right, honey?" he asked as best as he could through a broken jaw, trying desperately to unbuckle himself.

Delores heard Marion talking to her but she was too busy tending to herself. She touched the gash in her forehead and her fingers came away bloody. She rubbed her fingers together feeling the texture of the blood and then she looked to Marion. "I'm-I'm okay, sweetie. I'm-I'm gonna try to find my cell phone to call the police and then I'm gonna try to unbuckle you."

"Okay." He replied.

It took some time but Delores managed to unbuckle herself, and she hit the ceiling of the Jeep, wincing. She then unlocked the door but it wouldn't open. Acknowledging this, she kicked out the windshield, which had already been weakened by a crack that resembled a spider's cobweb. The broken glass caved in and fell on the ground as well on the inside of the truck. Crawling out, Delores ended up slicing her palm on a shard of glass. She howled in pain and pulled herself up on her good leg since her other leg had a sprung ankle. Looking down at her wound, she saw that it was bleeding, profusely. She tore off a length of her dressed and tied it around her hand, pulling it tight with her teeth.

Looking back inside of the Jeep, Delores spotted her cellular amongst the broken glass. She grabbed it and unlocked it. She had dialed nine-one, and then she stopped once she was about to press one again. At that time, a light bulb came on inside of her head and a wicked smile stretched across her face. Still holding her cell phone, she limped around the truck and got down on her knees before Marion. She sat the cellular aside, and pretended like she was going to unbuckle her husband. Instead, she reached inside of the broken out window on the driver side and placed both of her hands over his nose and mouth. She pressed down hard and turned her head, because she didn't want to look into his eyes. This was because she was afraid that if she did, his face would haunt her forever.

The only reason I was fucking witcho ass was because I was down on my luck and you was getting to the money. I ain't got no problems being the trophy wife just as long as you sponsoring a bitch. But the way I'm seeing things now, why juice yo' big baldheaded ass for years on out? Hell, I may as well get rid of you now so I can collect on that million dollar life insurance policy, Delores thought to herself as she held her hands over the lower half of Marion's face, feeling him struggling to stop her. He was a big strong dude, but the accident had left him weakened.

Once Delores felt Marion go slack, she peeked over at him and saw that he was dead. "'Bout time, goddamn, nigga, you wasn't tryna get up outta here, huh? Alright, now, where's my phone." Her eyes scanned the ground until she discovered her cellular. Picking it up, she unlocked it and dialed 9-1-1

26

again. Placing her hand to her mouth, she cleared her throat and prepared to put on an Oscar worthy performance as soon as someone picked up.

"Oh my God, please, help me! My husband and I have been in a really bad car accident and I think he's dead…" she went on talking as real, live tears came spilling down her cheeks and dripping off her chin. The bitch could star alongside Denzel with the acting chops she was displaying.

Shatira sat the portrait back down on the nightstand and snatched a few tissues from out of the Kleenex box. She wiped her eyes with the tissues and then blew her nose and wiped it. She then balled it up and threw it into the waste basket by the closet. Shatira's father was one of the biggest heroin dealers in Southern California. She expected him to get murdered in a drug war or spend the rest of his life behind bars, before she believed he'd die in a car accident. She didn't have any concrete evidence, but she believed beyond a reasonable doubt that her stepmother had murdered her father. She felt it in her gut, which was why she didn't trust her as far as she could see her.

Shatira hated the ground that her stepmother, Delores, walked on. She was mean, deceitful, abusive and arrogant, especially since she collected the million dollars on her father's life insurance policy. Like most people that grew up in poverty, Delores didn't know what to do with all of the money she'd inherited. Instead of buying a house in an upper class area where they all could be safe, the bitch copped a crib dead smack in the ghetto, where they could be touched over that paper she was sitting on. On top of that, she bought a GT Bentley. She was definitely drawing all of the wolves' attention in that luxury vehicle. There wasn't anyone else on the Eastside with a car that expensive, so she knew that people were checking for them.

Bitch is stupid with a capital S, buying that luxurious ass car and copping this raggedy ass pad. The fucking car costs more than the house. Like Dave Chapelle said, 'They should have never gave you niggaz money'. For real, for real, Shatira thought as she shook her head. *Bought all of those clothes, shoes, jewelry, big screen Tv's and the rest of that other unnecessary bullshit, just to stunt on the mothafuckaz that's living under the same circumstances as you. Dumb ass!*

Shatira allowed her thoughts to drift off to the double date she was going to go out on with Cee Cee, Flocka and Menace. She was ecstatic inside and couldn't wait. Her excitement had taken over her and she found herself falling back in bed, thrashing her arms and legs. She had a big old smile on her lips as she balled her pillow beneath her and thought about how fine Menace was. She was going to be sure to put on her best outfit that night. She wanted to let him see that she had crazy swag and sex appeal

Hold on, let's see what lil' momma got up in here to stunt on lil' daddy tonight," Shatira said to no one in particular. She bounced up off the bed and headed over to the closet. Smiling from ear to ear, she searched through the rack of her enormous wardrobe looking for her cutest outfit to wear that night.

Chapter Three

Flocka and Menace walked inside of The Drunken Monkey to find it considerably crowded. There were patrons laughing, talking, shooting pool, dancing and looking up at the monitors stationed at various sections of the establishment, while they partook in their respective alcohol beverages. A tune, the young niggaz weren't familiar with, played from the jukebox, which was at the center of the wall at the back of the room. Every so often they'd hear a pool ball clack into another pool ball as a shooter took his shot. Two barmaids crossed their lines of vision with platters of Buffalo wings and drinks. The wings were hot and spicy. Flocka loved spicy chicken wings. In fact, he made himself a mental note to try some one day.

Flocka looked to the bar and found the bartender, Mohamed, cleaning out a beer mug with a rag. He was a tall dude with a thin goatee and a long hair, which he wore pulled back in a braided ponytail. The man looked like he could have been from a third world country, like Saudi Arabia or some shit. Flocka stepped to the bar with Menace on his heels and motioned the bartender over with the wave of a twenty dollar bill. Seeing the money, the taller man came right over, still cleaning the mug out with a rag. The mothafucka didn't say a word though. He just threw his head back like *What's up?*

"I needa holla at that nigga Raffy."

Mohamed sat the mug down and snatched the bill out of Flocka's hand. He threw up one of his fingers and picked up a telephone that was secure behind the bar on the wall. He dialed up a number and placed one finger inside of his ear as he listened to the line ringing. He had done this because he knew the music was loud and so were the patrons that were there that night. Flocka and Menace looked around the bar as

29

they waited for Mohamed to wrap up his conversation. Before they knew it, he was hanging up the telephone and giving them directions to Raffy's office, which was towards the back of the bar, where the telephone booths were located.

"Good lookin' out." Flocka tapped his fist against his chest. He then nudged Menace and headed towards their destination. Once they reached the corridor, at the end of the hallway, they found the steps that led up to Raffy's office.

Flocka nudged Menace and they made their way down the hallway, past an older gentleman that was on the telephone. He glanced up at them, but he kept at his conversation on the telephone. Flocka and Menace made their way up the steps and knock on the door. Waiting, they could hear Raffy talking to someone on the telephone.

"Hold on for a sec', will ya? Someone's at the door." he told whoever he was on the jack with. He then projected his voice towards the door. "Who is it?"

"Flocka," he called out.

Buzzzz!

The black door buzzed and clicked unlock, it then swung open. Flocka and Menace crossed the threshold and entered the office. It had a black glow in the dark pool table with balls at the center of its floor, black leather couches, black leather massage chair and monitors on all four walls. Flocka and Menace found Raffy sitting behind his desk talking on his Blu-tooth. He was in a black button-up shirt and charcoal slacks. His black leather shoes were crossed and propped up on the desk top. Raphael or Raffy as he referred being called, was a bookie and loan shark. He was one of the biggest gangstas in West L.A. He made a lot of money and owned several businesses. He was a tall, slender man with slicked back hair and a five o'clock shadow.

Raffy looked up from his desk where he was jotting down something on a legal pad. He held up one finger for the young men to give him a minute and finished writing down whatever information he was receiving. Once he'd finished, he said goodbye and disconnected the call. He then went on writing something down on the legal pad, carrying on like he didn't see Flocka and Menace standing before him.

"This mothafucka ain't even gone acknowledge us?" Menace asked Flocka in a hushed tone.

"Fuck 'em! I'm just here to lay this cash on 'em, so we can get up outta here." Flocka responded and pulled a manila envelope from the back of his jeans. He approached the desk and tossed it upon it.

"My good friend, Flocka, I'm surprised you have the balls to show your face around here, especially with all of the marbles you owe me from your gambling debts." Raffy spoke as he continued to jot down on the legal pad, eyes focused on the page; Raffy had been doing business with Flocka for years. He paid him promptly whenever he placed a gambling bet. But recently the kid's luck had taken a turn for the worse and he'd been losing every bet he placed. This is when Raffy began to notice that the youth was taking longer and longer to pay his debts. Once he didn't come up with the five-hundred grand he was into him for, he shut down his tab and didn't allow him to place any more bets. Now normally he'd order someone to be beaten or murdered for not coughing up the cash they'd owed him, but he'd taken a liking to Flocka. It was because of this reason and this reason only, that he allowed him to keep his life and make payments. The deal was for Flocka to pay him at least forty grand a month, but so far the nigga had been coming up short. "I hope that's the full amount we agreed upon every month, because if it's not, I'm going to be pretty pissed off."

Raffy stopped writing and dropped his ink pen on the legal pad. He then snatched the manila envelope up and opened it. He didn't even bother to pull the money out of it and count it, because he knew that it wasn't forty stacks in there. All it took him was one glance inside of the envelope. Seeing that once again Flocka had come up short, Raffy turned red with anger and tossed it back upon his desk top.

"Ten G's? You're gonna have to do a lot better than that, my friend. You owe me a dinosaur's shit load of money."

"Yeah, I know, and you gon' get yours. I just need a lil' more time to put a few things together."

"You said that the last time you were here." Raffy reminded him, folding his hands in his lap and leaning back in his executive chair. He had a look on his face that said he was getting tired of Flocka's bullshit.

"Shit is rough out there. You know how it is when you're tryna to come up."

Raffy had shut his eyelids and began massaging the bridge of his nose when Flocka began talking. A second later, he looked up and said, "Right. And that's the only reason why I haven't sent a couple of my guys to break your kneecaps with steel pipes for your failure to pay me."

Flocka's forehead crinkled and his jaws tightened. A vein at the center of his forehead bulged with anger. "My nigga, watch how you talk to me, I ain't one of your flunkies. Show me the proper respect."

The Streets Don't Love Nobody

Raffy rose up from his chair and planted his hands down upon the desk top. He stared Flocka dead in his eyes as he talked to him. "Buddy, all my respect for you went out of the window when you started breaking your word on these payments. A man is only as good as his word, you know that shit! So don't start getting brand new on me now!"

"You tryna play me out in front of my man?" Flocka scowled and twisted up his lips.

"No. This is playing you out in front of your man." Raffy had sat back down and pressed a button beneath the edge of his desk. The buzzer sounded off and the door to his office opened. Six thug-ass niggaz filed inside over the threshold toting baseball bats, with crooked nails in them. Flocka and Menace went to draw their guns, but then they remembered that they'd left them inside of the car. This was because the bar had metal detectors. Unarmed, they were left at the baseball bat toting thugs' mercy.

The mean sons of bitches with the spiked baseball bats surrounded Flocka and Menace. As soon as Raffy gave them the order, they would beat the young niggaz into bloody ground beef.

Flocka and Menace looked around at all of the hard faces of the baseball bat wielding men, wondering what was about to go down.

"Remove all of your jewelry and place it on my desk top," Raffy commanded Flocka as he casually peeled a banana and took a bite out of it.

"You got me fucked up, homeboy!" Flocka spat furiously.

"Not yet, but as soon as I give my guys the word, they'll see to it that you and your friend are all of the way fucked up. Trust me." He munched on his banana with his jaws full.

When Raffy seen that Flocka wasn't budging to take off his jewelry, he gave his head bustas the nod to beat him and Menace to a bloody pulp. The head bustas stepped forward and raised their baseball bats.

"Wait!" Menace threw up his hand and the men looked to Raffy. He hesitantly gave the thug ass niggaz the nod, stopping theit bludgeoning of Flocka and his homeboy. "Give 'em yo' jewels, Flocka."

"Fuck that, Blood! The only way they gettin' my shit off me is if it's on my dead body. You Griff me?" Flocka looked around as he held his fist before his eyes, ready to throw down fighting for the shines round his neck.

Menace leaned closer to Flocka and said in a hushed tone, "Don't be stupid, bro. Them mothafucking chains and shit ain't worth our lives. That's material shit, you can get that back."

Flocka exhaled and thought on it for a minute. Realizing that his comrade was right, he relieved himself of his jewelry and placed it all on the desk top in front of Raffy. Raffy pulled the pile of jewelry closer to him and opened the drawer of his desk. He pulled out what looked like a handheld metal detector and waved it over the jewelry. The light on the device beeped and glowed blue, letting him know that the jewelry was indeed real.

Raffy nodded his approval of the authentic jewels. He looked over each piece of jewelry with a tool that jewelers use to check the clarity of diamonds. Afterwards, he pulled out a calculator and punched in some numbers. While he was doing this, Flocka and Menace exchanged confused glances. Once Raffy finished crunching digits, he took a deep breath and turned the calculator around to Flocka. He motioned the young nigga over and he approached, picking up the calculator.

"You owe me a total of $300,000 dollars. It was 330, but I like even dollar amounts. Well, that and I'm not a petty man." Flocka placed the calculator back on the desk top and slid it before Raffy. "I tell you what I'm going to do. I'm going to let chu walk out of here, and I'm going give you exactly two weeks. That's fourteen days," he showed him with his fingers. "You have fourteen days to come up with my money. If you don't then you die. I'm going to have my people skip torturing you, and just murder your black ass-betting ass." He smacked the desk top with his palm and balled his fist. He stared Flocka dead in his eyes, so that he'd know that he wasn't bullshitting him. "Get the fuck out of my office, now!"He pointed his finger at the door, demanding that Flocka and Menace leave. Afterwards, he picked his banana back up and spun around in his chair, giving his back to his guests.

Raffy continued to eat his banana, the presence of Flocka had sickened him.

***

Bump! Bunk! Beep! Dung!

Flocka punched on the steering wheel and accidentally beeped his vehicle's horn. He suddenly stopped and gripped the steering wheel. His chest jumped up and down as he breathed heavily. He was so pissed off that he was seeing red and he could feel his blood boiling.

"Fuuuuck, man! This foreign mothafucka took my jewels and shit! You know how I'ma look out here in these streets, huh?" Flocka looked to Menace who looked like he was in deep thought about something as he massaged his chin.

"You good, homeboy, you dealing with a sophisticated gangsta here. He's not some hood nigga that's gone have his young boys out here flossing yo' shit. If anything, he'll sit on 'em until you kick in the dough you owe 'em. Trust me. You'll be able to get cho shit back. Homie and his people ain't no jewel rockers like that. You Griff me?" he looked to him.

Flocka took a deep breath and ran his hands down his face. Having calmed himself down, he looked to his right-hand man and said, "Yeah, you probably right."

Menace gripped his shoulder and said, "We just gotta run a check up to pay this nigga off, so we can squash that gambling debt you got with 'em."

"We?" his brows furrowed.

"Yes, nigga, *we*. As in you and me. As long as yo' boy alive you don't ever have to face a problem by yo' self."

"That's love, dawg." He cracked a smile, displaying his gold teeth.

"That's what I got for you, my nigga." Menace dapped him up. "Now, let's get the fuck up from outta here."

With that having been said, Flocka cranked his old school up and peeled off. Not long after, Menace's cellular phone rang and he answered, seeing *Big Meat* on the screen.

"Yo' this the OG," Menace told Flocka before he answered the call. He listened attentively to what he was being told and then disconnected the call. "Yo', he wants us ASAP, nigga talking about code red and shit. Turn this mothafucka around and jump on the 105."

"Alright." Flocka mashed on the brakes and busted a U-turn in the middle of the street, heading back in the other direction.

Chapter Four

After her shower Shatira stepped out of the tub and snatched her towel from off the rack. She took the time to dry her hair and body before wrapping the towel around her. Stepping before the medicine cabinet's fogged mirror, she wiped a clear space in it until she was able to see her reflection. She couldn't wait to go on her double date that night with Menace. Just the thought of finally getting to hang out with him had her smiling from ear to ear. To tell the truth, she wasn't even that psyched about going to the movies. They could have been doing something as boring as watching paint dry for all she cared. Long as she was going to be able to be around him it didn't matter to her.

Although the thought of chilling with Menace had her on cloud nine, Shatira was still kind of worried about her stepmother. She wasn't eighteen yet, so she'd still have to ask for her permission to go out, but she wasn't even about to ask her. She already knew the answer to that question and it was 'hell no'. It wasn't like she was a bad child or anything. In fact, she was a damn good kid. She didn't get into any trouble, she was a homebody, she made good grades in school and she stayed to herself, mostly. Her stepmother, Delores, was just an evil wicked bitch that didn't want anyone to have fun unless it was herself or her punk ass identical twins

Shatira believed that her stepmother hated her, but for what reasons, she didn't have a clue. She often wondered why, but she never came up with any answers so she just left things be. The way she saw it, things were just how they were and they weren't going to change unless her stepmother wanted them to

Whatever! I'm just glad her evil ass is gone for the night. She shouldn't be back 'til two-thirty or three o'clock.

38

The Streets Don't Love Nobody

She normally stays out all night dancing and drinking with the rest of her wretched ass friends. That should give me more than enough time to see the movie and grab a bite to eat afterwards. Shiiiit, that bitch told me to wash the dishes and mop! Fuck that! I gotta get ghost in a minute. I'm not tryna miss this date for nobody. My boo gon' be there, and I know he gon' be looking fiiiiiine, Shatira thought as she did a little dance, snapping her fingers and moving her body to the beat playing inside of her head.

***

Blam! Blam! Blam!

Slugs hit the ground near his dirty boots and sent debris into the air. Feeling the hot ones so close to him jacked his heart rate up. The frightened young man thought he was doing a good job of dodging the bullets by tucking his head and zig zagging, but little did he know the gunman was only toying with him. As he was leading him into the direction that he wanted him to go.

"Haa! Haa! Haa! Haa!" He breathed heavily, beads of sweat oozing out of the pores on his forehead, running as fast as he could and occasionally glancing over his shoulders at the trio of jeeps on him like stink of shit.

"Oh God, please, don't let 'em catch me!" he spoke to no one in particular, moving past trees. He was in the final hour of his life, and the only thing that could save him short of a miracle from God was a deal with the Devil.

"Haa! Haa! Haa! Haa!" homie moved like he had a lynch mob behind him.

Snap! Crack! Packkk!

The thin branches and twigs snapped and scratched up his face, arms and legs. His adrenaline was pumping just as fast as his heart and his body felt hot. He couldn't feel the cuts and bruises his running through the trees had caused. Hell naw, he was too focused on losing these niggaz that were on his ass. He was moving so quickly that he looked like a blur in the woods. As bad as he wanted to stop and catch a breather he couldn't. He knew that if the Top Dawg caught up with him that there was going to be hell to pay.

"You makin' a real bad mistake makin' me come after you like this, Coolie. All you doin' is raisin' my blood pressure and pissin' me the fuck off, " Big Meat spoke through a mega phone, as he hung from the side of the jeep, his massive hand clutching a Desert Eagle. He was dressed in camouflage like the rest of his goons, with a rifle slung over his shoulder. His big bald head, which had skin bunched at the top of it, shined under the rays of the blazing sun. He was a dark-skinned man with a wide nose and a square jaw. His broad shoulders were the perfect match to his body builder's physique.

Big Meat was the boss of a family that was said to be as powerful as the Italian mafia. He was knee deep in organized crime. He had his hands in everything from extortion to pimping. And if you wanted to make money on his side of town doing anything illegal, you had better come up with your taxes or that was your ass.

Big Meat had invited Coolie out to the woods to hunt some game. Little did Coolie know, he was the game. By the time he realized what was going on, Big Meat and his goons were ringing shots at him, and he was running through the trees like he was a deer or some shit.

The Streets Don't Love Nobody

Coolie threw his head back and ran harder, legs covering ground quicker than he could imagine. Stepping on a stone partially hidden within the dirt caused him to slip and twisted his ankle. "Huuu!" He grimaced as he fell awkwardly and hit the surface on his side. Shaking the pain from his mental, he looked behind him and saw the jeeps closing in on him. "Oh shit!" His eyes got as big as saucers and worry lines etched across his forehead. Terrified, he hobbled upon his good leg and glanced at his rear. Behind him, he found the first jeep pulling to a stop which was carrying a very heated Big Meat. The other two jeeps came to a stop on either side of the arriving jeep. The refrigerator sized man known as Big Meat jumped down on the ground and calmly strolled towards his target.

"Oh, God, no!" Coolie's heart raged inside of his chest seeing Big Meat with the shiny chrome gun. The sunlight kissed off the deadly weapon and caused it to gleam brightly for a moment's time. Realizing that his life was in grave danger, Coolie hurried along as fast as he could on one leg, but then he felt something hot pierce the calf of his last functioning limb. Flames engulfed leg and he winced, meeting the ground face first. When he pulled his face back up it was masked by dirt. Hearing the footfalls of Big Meat's booted feet as he approached, he tried to crawl forward, clawing at the dirt. Seeing this, the big man popped two shots into his thighs causing him to howl in pain. When Coolie turned over he had a face masked by excruciation. He could have died when he saw Big Meat advancing in his direction with his gun pointed at him.

"Fuck is my ends!" Big Meat's frightful eyes bored into his victim's eyes. He was gripping his weapon so tight that his hand turned white at the knuckles.

"I-I-I didn't take yo' money, Meat. Man, I swear to…"

Coolie cut himself short squeezing his eyelids shut when the big man leaned forward. He thought he was about to shoot him in his face, but when he felt his hand inside of his pocket his eyes peeled back open, confused. He found him standing back erect with his goons on either side of him, menacing expressions plastered across their faces.

Big Meat peeled off each bills of the wad he'd just pulled out of Coolie's pocket, counting them off. There was a total of five thousand dollars.

"So, this paypa ain't mine, right? It don't belong to me?" Big Meat's jeweled hand held up the dead presidents.

"No, no." Eyes bulging with terror, Coolie shook his head rapidly. "I would never bite the hand that feeds me, Meat! You gotta believe me, man! You've gotta believe me!" His eyes misted with tears and they came sliding down his cheeks, as his bottom lip trembled. "Please, please, please, don't kill me, man!"

"Shut the fuck up, you lyin' ass nigga!" Bumpy scowled, pointing his .9mm at his head. He was a older nigga that sported his hair in a close fade and gray stubble was formed his goatee. Bumpy was Big Meat's right-hand man and enforcer. He made his name back in the day snatching bodies and dumping on anyone opposing a threat to the organization that he pledged his allegiance to.

"On my momma rest in peace, Bumpy, I'm not lyin', fam." Coolie whimpered.

"That bitch turnin' over in her grave right now." Bumpy countered, looking down at him like he was shit at the bottom of his shoe.

The Streets Don't Love Nobody

"Let me show you something, youngsta." Big Meat kneeled down to Coolie and showed him the corners of a couple of the bills he'd taken from out of his pocket. Once he had his full attention, Big Meat pointed to what appeared to be S's at the corners of the bills. "You see those tiny S's at the corners of each of these bills? Well, they're not really S's. Nah, they're snakes and I drew them there myself," Coolie's eyes grew big and a wet spot began to expand at his crotch. He knew that his ass was in for it now. "So, I'd know exactly who the snake was in the family." He snarled and spat a glob of off yellow phlegm into Coolie's face. It splattered against his forehead just as he squeezed his eyelids closed. The thick goo dripped off of his brow. He then wiped it away with the back of his hand.

"Sssssss! Sssssss! Sssssss!" All of the goons made the sounds of hissing snakes, staring down at Coolie like the hoe ass nigga that he was. His head darted up and down the rows of faces surrounding him. Terror etched across his face and he swallowed the ball of nervousness in his throat.

"Please, Meat, man, please," he put his trembling hands together in prayer. "My son needed some formula and…"

Wamp!

The big man kicked him so hard in the face that it split his forehead head open and caused blood to ooze. The wounded man looked up at him dazed and confused, head bobbling about.

"Fuck that lil' nigga, he ain't my son!" Big Meat growled angrily, gritting and tossing the money down on him. "Which one of them hands you use to steal from me, pussy?"

he holstered his Desert Eagle and unsheathed a machete from around his back, flipping it over in his palm.

"Come…come…come on, man…" he tried to speak but the blow to his forehead had him hurting and discombobulated. "I…"

Big Meat's head snapped to Bumpy, "This nigga a left or right handed?"

"Left handed," He responded, eyes focused on the disloyal member of their organization.

"Fun fact, did you know in third world country's they hack off whichever hand that the thief was caught stealing with?"

Without hesitation, Big Meat grabbed his victim by his wrist and yanked his arm forward. As Coolie was coming to the realization of what was going on it was already too late.

"Wai…"

Sniktttt!

The blade went through the disloyal man's limb like a hot knife through butter, and blood squirted from his stump. Veins bulged up his neck and temples as his mouth stretched wide open, unleashing a scream so loud that it sent the birds flying from out of the trees.

The goons didn't even flinch. They'd become accustomed to this kind of brutality from their boss.

"Arghhhhhhhhh!"

Shortly, Coolie went into shock. His eyes crossed and his mouth quivered uncontrollably, his stump moving about, animatedly. The sound was zapped out of his voice box and he fell back against the surface.

While this was going on, Flocka and Menace were pulling up in his Chevrolet Impala. They frowned seeing their boss chop off one of his most loyal soldiers arm. Quickly, they threw open their respective doors and hopped out, en route to where all of the action was unfolding. They stopped once they were close enough to get a good look at the show.

After hacking off Coolie's arm, Big Meat whipped around holding up the severed limb; its blood sprawling down his arm and dripping off of his elbow. He casted his dark eyes at all of the niggaz that were a part of *The Family.* This was his way of letting them know that if they were ever disloyal to him that the same thing could happen to them, maybe even worse.

"You see this? You see this, huh?" Big Meat wagged the limp arm, disturbing its fingers. "This is what happens when you steal from me! Stealing shall never be tolerated in this family! It's against the law, and it's a violation punishable by death!" he tossed the severed arm aside and gave Bumpy a nod. This was a signal for him to pop a round into sticky fingers A.K.A Coolie. That's exactly what he did. Once he was done, everyone else took their turn, putting a hot one in his thieving ass. The last one to put a bullet in him was Big Meat.

"Aaaaaah, fuck, ahhh, they hot! These fucking bullets are hot!" Coolie complained as he grimaced and cradled his bleeding stump.

Feeling the presence of two more parties, Big Meat looked over his shoulder to find Flocka and Menace. He motioned for the two young niggaz to come over with a throw of his head and they obliged him. They already knew what needed to be done. They all had to go through with putting some hot shit in the traitor. This way, anyone thinking about talking to the cops would also be telling of their own involvement in the murder as well.

Flocka took the .9mm from his boss' hand and pointed it at Coolie, turning it sideways. He scowled and shook his head thinking of how pitiful the nigga was lying at his feet. Without a second thought, he popped one into that nigga'z shoulder. The bullet ripped through his shoulder and blood splattered out of the back of it, staining the ground. Menace was next up, taking the gun into his hand. He stepped up and stood over the thief, looking down at him with pity. He and old boy had grown pretty close over the years. It was safe to say that he considered him a friend.

"Put him out of his misery, son." Big Meat urged Menace.

Big Meat looked back and forth between Menace and Coolie, as he wiped his crimson stained hand on the shirt of one of his men, using his shirt like it was a towel. He couldn't help wondering if Menace was going to off him or not. If he refused to go through with nodding him, then he was going to put on in his head and leave his men with twice the work. Meaning, they were going to have to bury two bodies instead of one.

"Come on, Menace, stall me out, man, we 'pose to be boys!'" Coolie whined, tears flooding his cheeks.

"Fuck all of that shit, Menace my mothafuckin' homeboy. You know the rules, you stole from the family and now yo' bitch ass gots ta pay." Flocka said, standing beside Menace, staring down at the nigga that he had to pop.

"That's right," Big Meat threw his arm over Menace's shoulders. "Gon' and end this faggot, so we can bury 'em."

"Menace, man, pleas…"

Bloc! Bloc! Bloc! Bloc!

Menace splattered that fuck-nigga'z noodle, leaving what looked like hamburger meat and pasta sauce on the ground. Big Meat whipped out a rag from his back pocket and told Menace to place the murder weapon inside of it. He did like he was told and Big Meat wrapped the gun up in the rag, tucking it at the small of his back.

"Y'all bury this mothafucka six feet in the ground so we can get up outta here!" Big Meat commanded his men.

"Alright, y'all heard the man, let's get to work." Bumpy told the goons. He then reached inside of the Jeep and tossed two shovels to the men so they could star digging. While he was busy doing this, the other goons were taking shovels out of the other jeeps to that they could with the digging of the grave.

Big Meat turned his attention to Menace and Flocka, dapping them up. "So, what' up, youngstas? What y'all been up to today?"

"Ain't shit, big dawg, movin' and shakin'." Flocka told him.

"How 'bout chu, champ?" Big Meat smiled and threw playful punches at Menace which he countered with playful punches of his own. The big man then threw his arm around Menace's shoulders and continued his conversation. "Look, y'all know Darnell, right?"

"I know of 'em?" Flocka said.

"I seen 'em around." Menace replied.

"Ok, good. Familiarity." Big Meat said. "Well, I need y'all to go on his rounds with 'em. You know, picking up the paypa niggaz owe me and shit? He's had a problem with collecting from Ricky's spot. Seems there was a thief that was cutting into homeboy's earnings, which means he was cutting into my share as well. Anyway, I want chu two to ride along with 'em to make sure shit runs smooths. Should y'all run into any problems, well, I don't have to say. 'Cause y'all know how my hittas do, right?" he looked between Flocka and Menace. They both nodded. "Alright then. That's all a nigga wanted, y'all can gon' 'bout cha business. I'll have Darnell hit y'all with the time and place."

Flocka and Menace dapped up Big Meat and made their departure.

Chapter Five

That night

Shatira lay in bed pretending to be asleep. Her eyes slowly peeled open and she looked at the digital clock on her nightstand. It had just turned 9 o'clock. Right then, she sprung from out of her bed, fully clothed. She was wearing a white V-neck, which she wore underneath a black leather vest, leather bell bottom pants and high heel boots. Shatira rushed over to the mirror residing over her nightstand and popped open her jewelry box. She took out a pair of small platinum diamond earrings and fixed them in her ears. Next, she pulled the scarf free from her head and her long black silky hair fell over her shoulders and face, making her look like Uncle Fester. Afterwards, she shook her head from left to right, causing her hair to swing in either direction. Having stood in the mirror fluffing it out, she picked her most expensive perfume from off the nightstand and sprayed some into the air. Tilting her head back, she allowed the mist to fall upon her. She then sprayed a little of the perfume on her wrists, capped the bottle and sat it down on the nightstand.

After getting prepared for the night, Shatira texted Menace to let him know that she was ready. She then opened her bedroom door and snuck out into the hallway, looking into Delores' bedroom. She found her stepmother asleep under the covers with the television's light dancing across her face. After shutting her stepmother's bedroom door, Shatira snuck back inside of her bedroom and pushed open the window. Peeking over the ledge, she saw that she was two stories up, but she was sure she could make it down. Climbing out of the window, Shatira held onto the ledge and allowed herself to hang for a moment, looking down over her shoulder.

Tranay Adams

Okay, girl, here goes nothing, Shatira thought to herself and released the ledge. She managed to grab one of the branches of a tree just below her window, but her hands slipped free of it, delaying her fall. Glancing down, the ground appeared to be rising towards her fast. Before Shatira knew it, she was crashing to the ground, wincing.

"Aaah! I think a bitch done broke her ass bone," Shatira said with her face scrunched up, rubbing her behind. Hearing laughter, she looked up and saw Flocka's Impala. He and Cee Cee were in the front seat laughing their asses off, while a silhouette was moving toward her. The closer it got the more of the person's features filled out. It was Menace. Her wore a concerned look on his face as he extending his hand out to her.

"You okay, slim?" Menace asked Shatira as he pulled her upon her feet. Having hold of both her hands, he stared into her eyes as she smiled, happily.

"Yeah-well, now that you're here." She capped as she blushed.

He licked his lips and smiled, too. "Check you out. I'm 'pose to be the nigga that delivers all of the smooth lines and shit."

"I guess I beat chu to the punch, huh?"

Honkk! Honkkkk!

Menace and Shatira looked in the direction of the blaring car horn. They found Cee Cee hanging halfway out of the passenger window, motioning for them to come on.

"Come on, ya'll, we gon' mess around and be late for the movies!" Cee Cee called out to them.

The Streets Don't Love Nobody

A frowning Shatira stomped her foot and said through gritted teeth, "Bitch, keep yo' mothafucking voice down for my wicked ass stepmother hears you."

"Oops, my bad," Cee Cee smacked her hand over her mouth and blushed with embarrassment.

"Come on," Shatira took her future boo by the hand and led him toward the '64. She limped along rubbing her butt.

Goddamn that shit hurt, a wincing Shatira thought.

Shatira and Menace climbed inside of the Chevy Impala and slammed the doors shut, simultaneously. Right after, Flocka pulled off down the street.

"What's up, Flocka?" Shatira reached up front and patted him on his shouler.

"'Sup with it?" Flocka said, looking up at Shatira through the rearview mirror, smirking.

"Ain't nothing. Just glad to be out the house," she admitted.

"Heyyyy, boo," Cee Cee turned around in the seat smiling at her homegirl, chewing gum. "I see you managed to escape prison."

"Yeah. It wasn't easy and I know it will be hell to pay should I get caught. I just hope it's well worth it." she smiled at Menace. This caused him to smile and interlock his fingers with hers. He brought her hand to his lips and kissed it tenderly, staring into her eyes. Shatira blushed and her stomach fluttered with butterflies. She was crazy about the young nigga.

"Menace, look how you got my girl, all googly eyed and shit," Cee Cee looked from Menace to Shatira who was trying to hide her smile. Cee Cee acknowledging that her best friend was smitten by Menace caused her smile harder.

The illumination from the light posts flashed on and off of everyone's faces as the Impala sped through the streets. The windows were open so the air blew inside, disturbing their hair and ruffling their clothing. "Look at my boo, she's smitten by you. What chu do to my girl, man?"

"I ain't do nothing, just being me," Menace looked to Shatira and saw her smiling hard, covering her face with her other hand. She hated herself for not being able to confine her feelings.

"Yeah, well, I can tell you right now that the pussy is dripping wet in them leopard print panties of hers. You ain't even gotta work for 'em them bitches gone slide right off." Cee Cee said, sitting back down in her seat.

Hearing her bestie say this, Shatira looked down and saw that her leopard printed panties were visible. She lifted up off the seat and pulled her leather pants upon her waist.

"Cee Cee, please, you don't even know what the fuck you talking about."

"Whatever," Cee Cee threw up her hand dismissing Shatira's claims. She knew her bestie like she knew the back of her hand. And by the way she was carrying on, her pussy has to be wet.

A smirk came across Menace's lips.

He didn't know what to say so he kept his mouth shut.

The Streets Don't Love Nobody

"Bitch, why don't chu shut up? Damn, you talk too much!" Shatira shook her head, smiling. The smile on her face was counterfeit though. Cee Cee had blown up her spot and she was trying to hide her embarrassement. You see, she wanted to check Cee Cee's ass for putting her out there like that, but she didn't want to change the playful atmosphere and ruin the night.

"Whatever, hoe, you feeling that nigga," Cee Cee looked up in the rearview mirror and stuck her tongue out at her. She chuckled once she saw Shatira smirk and give her the finger.

Cee Cee looked to Flocka and smiled, grabbing the bulge in his jeans. When Flocka felt her grasp his manhood, he looked over at her and smiled. Seeing that he was receptive to her, Cee Cee slid closer to him and licked his earlobe with the tip of her tongue. She then sucked on it and caressed his thigh. Before he knew it, she was kissing and nibbling on his neck 'causing him to narrow his eyelids into slit and bite down on his bottom lip.

While Cee Cee worked her magic on Flocka, he glanced up into the rearview mirror into the backseat. Through the reflection, he saw Menace and Shatira leaned up against one another, drifting off to sleep. Right then, he surfed the channels on his stereo until he found a song he was feeling. When he came across Tyrese's *Baby Boy,* he cranked the volume up and the singer's melodic voice came bursting through the speakers.

I know sometimes it might get crazy

I'll always be here for you lady

Baby, I'm just tryin'a change the game

Tranay Adams

So let me work the thang

Let me do my thing

After confirming the love birds were asleep, Flocka looked to Cee Cee and gave her a nod. Smiling, she took the gum from out of her mouth and brought it towards his lips, sticking it inside of his mouth. She then unzipped his jeans and pulled his meat from out of its denim prison. Cee Cee tucked her feet underneath her ass and leaned over into his lap, stroking his dick. While she was jacking him, she looked up to find him smiling and chewing the gum she'd given him. He glanced at her and then focused his attention back out of the windshield.

Cee Cee skillfully licked Flocka underneath his dick all the way up to its head, encircling it with her warm, wet tongue. By this time, the young gangsta ass nigga had a full hard-on, riddled with veins. Pre-cum slid out of Flocka's pee-hole and left a wet trail behind it. Cee Cee didn't give a fuck though. Nah, the bitch was a champion. She slid his entire wang inside of her moist, piping hot mouth. Cee Cee brought her thick lips up and down his dick, hard and passionately. Her saliva spilled down his dick, but she kept on sucking him off.

Cee Cee's slurping and sucking sounds grew louder and louder, filling the interior of the old school drop. Her mouth was feeling good as fuck to Flocka, but little momma was just a little too loud. Acknowledging this, the young gangta turned the volume up on the stereo. He then lay back in the seat holding the steering wheel with one hand and holding the back of Cee Cee's neck with the other. His eyelids fluttered and he licked his lips, biting down on his bottom one. He gasped louder and louder as he enjoyed Cee Cee's amazing mouth. By the look on Flocka's face, you would have thought he was possessed by an evil spirit.

54

The Streets Don't Love Nobody

Cee Cee pulled out his slightly hairy nut sack and massaged it, while she continued to suck him harder and faster. Her eyelids narrowed into slits as she handled her business. Her hums and groans sounded sexy as fuck to him, pushing him closer to his nut. Feeling the head of his dick enlarging and his sack swelling, Cee Cee knew that homie was about to blow his load. Looking down at her, Flocka's eyelids narrowed and his mouth formed an O. Little momma had some bomb ass head. That shit was undeniable.

"I'm about to bust," Flocka said in a hoarse voice. He went to move her head from off his dick, but she smacked his hand away and continued sucking him off. "Yo', ma, I'm 'bouta nut."

"Nut in my mouth, baby…nut in my mothafucking mouth," Cee Cee urged him, with a mouth full of his dick massaging his nut sack.

"Nasty ass, bitch, suck my dick! Suck my mothafuckin' dick!" Scowling and gritting, Flocka looked back and forth between the windshield and the back of Cee Cee's head. While he was doing this, he was jabbing his dick in and out of her mouth. This caused her to make gagging noises and tears spilled out of her eyes. "Aaaaaah, fuck!" He threw his head back for a moment and hollered. He then glanced down at Cee Cee continuing to jab her mouth. "Sssssss, I'm finna nut! I'm finna buts all in yo' mothafuckin' mouth! Here it comes! Here it comes! Aaaaah!" Flocka roared as he busted off, shooting his warm creamy goo into the roof of Cee Cee's mouth and coating her tongue. Looking back and forth between her and the windshield, he kept right along jabbing her mouth. He didn't stop until he'd drained his nut sack inside of her mouth.

"Whoooo!" Flocka smiled happily, having gotten himself off.

Cee Cee pulled her head up from Flocka's lap and showed him her mouth. It was full of his semen. She looked him dead in his eyes as she swallowed it like an Asprin. Smiling at him, she sucked her fingers as if his jizz was delicious.

Flocka flashed her a smile as he put his dick up and zipped up his jeans. He then leaned over and popped open the glove box. He grabbed a handful of napkins and passed them to Cee Cee.

"Thanks, boo," Cee Cee said as she took the napkins. She used the napkins to wipe the corners of her mouth and then she balled them up, throwing them out of the window. Opening the sun visor, she took a look at herself in the rectangle shaped glass mirror. She took a good look at her teeth to see if there was anything there like, Flocka's pubic hairs. There wasn't anything. Seeing this, she shut the sun visor and pulled out a Listerine strip from a small container inside of her handbag. Having popped the minty green strip inside of her mouth, she closed the handbag and sat it between her legs on the floor.

Cee Cee looked over her shoulder into the backseat; Menace and Shatira were still knocked out, asleep. She then turned her attention back to Flocka and smiled, saying, "Soooooo."

"Sooooooo, what?" Flocka grinned, looking from her to the windshield.

The Streets Don't Love Nobody

"Don't play with me, boy, you know what I'm getting at," Cee Cee playfully punched him in his arm. He looked at her with a silly look on his face.

"Oh, riiiight, my fault…the head. That shit was cool, I liked it." He admitted, nodding his head.

"Pretty cool? That's all I get?" Cee Cee's brows furrowed. She couldn't believe that he thought her head was just okay. She'd been told on several occasional by niggaz that her head game was legendary.

Flocka chuckled and said, "Nah, lil' momma, shit was fiyah. You know a nigga gotta always play the cool role and shit." He glanced back and forth between her and the windshield.

"You sho'? 'Cause I could always give it another shot." She smiled at him seductively as she toyed with the zipper of her jeans.

"Oh, I'm fa sho', fa sho'," he assured her. "But, uh, if you not too sure of yourself, then when we get up here to the theater, you can always redeem yourself." He caressed the side of Cee Cee's face and peeled her bottom lip down. She tilted her head down and eyed him hungrily, licking his thumb. She then grasped his wrist and sucked on his thumb slowly and then slightly faster, sensually. This caused his manhood to stiffen in his jeans.

"Why wait, when I can do that now?" Cee Cee smiled as she unzipped his jeans and dipped her head below his waistline. Once she sprung his dick free, she blessed him with her gift once again.

***

57

Menace, Flocka, Cee Cee and Shatira ended up at AMC theaters out in Torrance. They decided to see *Straight Outta Compton* since that seemed to be the big fuss on black Twitter and in the streets. After getting the snacks and food they planned to indulge in that night, they headed over to theater 5 and entered through the double doors. They rounded the corner nearing a light that appeared to be growing brighter and brighter as they approached. Before they knew it they were inside of the theater. The silver screen had commercials playing on it at the time; its illumination shone on the few people that were seated before the screen. The movie goers were either talking amongst one another, looking through their cell phones or making out.

"Where y'all tryna sit?" Menace asked Shatira, Flocka and Cee Cee.

"We gon' take the seats up in the nose bleeds?" Cee Cee spoke for herself and Flocka, pointing up high to the very top row of seats. The row was just below the window where the projector was cast out of to project the film that they were there to see.

Shatira's forehead crinkled when she looked up at the row of seats at the very top of the theater. "How the fuck y'all gon' see the movie from way up there?" she pointed to plenty of seats around them that they could sit in. "Look at all of these seats out here; they're much better than being wayyyy up there. Shit, you may as well have stayed at home and got chu a mothafucking bootleg."

Cee Cee leaned in closer to her homegirl and said in a hushed tone, "Bitch, if you don't shut cho dick suckers. I'm tryna work this nigga and you gon' fuck it up."

The Streets Don't Love Nobody

"I swear to God, Fee, youz a hoe." Shatira shook her head, laughing.

"Whatever 'cause Menace is gon' have yo' legs cocked open tonight, pumping and sweating between 'em. So, don't try to do me." She smiled. "I'll see you later, trick." She dapped her up and led Flocka up the burgundy carpeted steps toward the top row of seats.

Menace and Flocka exchanged glances and slight grins.

Menace and Shatira sat in the middle row of the theater, stuffing their faces with pop corn and other junk food. They then shared a big ass fountain drink of strawberry Fanta and Sprite mixed which was Shatira's favorite beverages. Afterwards, they held hands and watched the movie excitedly, Shatira with her head leaned on her date's shoulder. Occasionally, Menace would glance up at the top row. The very first time, he saw Flocka with his head back and his arms stretched across the seats on either sides of him. Seconds later, his body jerked violently and Cee Cee sat up wiping her mouth with the back of her hand. She looked down the rows of seats and cracked a grin, not giving a fuck about Menace seeing her suck off his boy. When Menace looked back up there later, Cee Cee was facing the silver screen and holding the arms of either seats beside her, sliding up and down Flocka's dick.

"What chu looking at?"Shatira asked Menace, catching him off.

"Nothing. I was just seeing what cha girl and the homie were doing." Menace said, focusing his attention back on the screen and taking a sip from their fountain drink

"And?"

"Shit, watching the movie like us." He passed her the fountain drink and kissed her on the forehead.

"For real? Knowing how Cee Cee gets down, I'm surprised they weren't fucking." She leaned her head back against his arm and focused back on the movie.

Sneakily, Menace glanced over his shoulder again, and sure enough, Cee Cee was still riding his boy, Flocka. Flocka threw up his fist in salute to his right-hand man and Menace cracked a grin. He gave him a slight nod and turned his attention back on the movie.

After the movie, the clan dipped to Fat Burger. They dined inside, eating and chopping it up about the movie. Well, Shatira and Menace did for the most part, because Flocka and Cee Cee only saw like the first fifteen to twenty minutes of the film, since they seated in the nose bleeds getting busy.

Once everyone had finished their food, they wrapped up their conversation and hopped on the freeway to head back home.

***

Menace and Shatira said their goodbyes to Flocka and Cee Cee. As the '64 Impala pulled off at the back of them, they walked off towards Shatira's house, hand in hand. Once they made it to the front door, Shatira turned around to Menace, smiling and blushing.

"Thanks for the night. I had a ball," Shatira told him.

The Streets Don't Love Nobody

"Me, too, we gotta paint the town red again some time," Menace smiled and bit down on his bottom lip. Once again, he was giving her that sexy look of his.

"Most def'," she smiled harder and threw her arms around his neck. She looked him in his eyes as she rubbed the tip of her nose against his and kissed him, romantically. She then broke her embrace and kissed him on the lips, one last time. "Call me tomorrow?"

"Oh, fa sho'," he kept eye contact with her as he held her hand, kissing it tenderly. He then walked off the steps and headed to his home, which was next door to hers.

Shatira opened the front door and closed it back, quietly. Removing her shoes, she then tip toed up the staircase as silently as she could. She made it past her stepmother's bedroom as well as her stepbrothers' bedroom. Once she was inside of her own bedroom, she disrobed and slid into bed under the covers. She had just shut her eyelids when she heard her cell phone vibrating on the nightstand, where she'd left it when she'd started getting undressed. When she looked at the screen, she smiled seeing that she had a text from Menace. It said *gn*, which meant goodnight. She responded back with *gn* and a kissy face emoji. Afterwards, she snuggled up against her pillow and shut her eyelids, drifting off to sleep.

Chapter Six

An hour later

The bedroom was dark as Shatira lie in bed asleep, a pleasant smile on her face as she dreamt about her and Menace's second date. He'd just walked her upon the porch of her house and was leaning in for a goodbye kiss when lightning struck.

Wap!

Shatira shot up in bed grimacing as a stinging sensation engulfed her mouth, grill filling with blood. She blinked rapidly trying to figure out what the hell had happened, touching her lips and coming away with bloody finger tips. The last thing she remembered was texting Menace and falling asleep. The next minute, she was being woken up by a punch to the mouth. Shatira spat off to the side, blood hanging from her bottom lip. Once she was able to focus, she saw her stepmother standing over her. The light from the hallway casted on her back and outlined her silhouette. Even through the darkness Shatira could make out her menacing stare. Her stomach twisted into knots and she felt queasy, like she was about to vomit. She glanced at her bed to see if her cellular was laid out in plain view. Thankfully, she didn't see it so she knew that the slap wasn't for her having a cell phone.

"Yo' lil' fast ass think you slick, huh? Sneaking outta the house to hang with them thug ass niggaz! Get cho mothafucking ass outta this bed!" Delores screamed on her, eyebrows arched and top lip trembling, angrily.

Shatira frowned up as she wiped her bleeding lip with the back of her hand. Her eyes shifted to the bedroom door and she saw her stepbrothers crowding it, snickering like a couple of kids. She was 38 hot, but knew that if she put hands on her stepmother that she'd definitely kick her out of the house. She feared being out in the streets with nowhere to go.

"What're you talking about? I been here all night," Shatira looked at her like she was crazy, continuously wiping the blood from her lip.

"Youz an ol' lying ass bitch! I got eyes and ears everywhere, you can't play me, hoe!" Delores smacked Shatira across her face, whipping her head and hair to the right. She then grabbed her by her hair and threw her down to the floor. Next, she punched her in her head and kicked her, repeatedly. Shatira tried to curl into a fetal position, but Delores grabbed a fistful of her hair and pulled her up.

"Arhhhhhh!" Shatira shrieked and grabbed her by her wrist. Pain shot through her scalp as her wicked stepmother dragged her out of her bedroom, kicking and screaming.

"You gon' learn today, hoe! I bet cha that!" Delores swore, her face twisted with hatred. "Y'all move! Get the fuck outta the way!" she swung her hand off to the side at her sons blocking the doorway. LaRon and Levon got the fuck up out of the way, not trying to feel their mother's wrath.

Delores drug Shatira down the hallway, steadily kicking and screaming, trying her best to escape the evil woman's grasp. The twins trailed behind them watching in amusement, smirks plastered on their lips. When Delores made it to the staircase, she dragged her stepdaughter down the staircase, causing her to bump her knees. Shatira grimaced and struggled to break loose, but her efforts were useless against the older woman's iron-grip.

"You think you gon' live up in my house rent free, witcho mothafucking feet up? Unh unh, you gotta 'notha thang coming, sweetheart!" Delores pulled Shatira inside of the kitchen. She and her sons stood over her. LaRon and Levon stood at her back, towering over her, making her look like a midget. "You know what, lil' Miss Hot-in-the-pants? You haven't been punished enough, not nearly enough. But that's about to change. Oh, yeah, that's about to change." She wagged her finger down at Shatira, as she held her head wincing. "LaRon, Levon, y'all want some pussy?"

"Fa sho'," Levon said, rubbing his hands together and staring down at Shatira, with hungry eyes. His brother, LaRon, was standing beside him licking his lips, thirstily. They couldn't wait to run up in that virgin pussy.

"Gon' and get some of them walls, boys," Delores oldered the twins as she stepped aside, smiling sinisterly.

"Well, seeing as how I'm the man of the house, I'll go first," Levon smacked Shatira around until she was dizzy. He then unzipped his jeans and straddled her. He tore open her shirt and her bra padded breasts were revealed. Next, he pinned her wrists down and began sucker on her neck.

Shatira whipped her head from left to right as she struggled to get up from the linoleum. Her tearing eyes snapped open and she screamed bloody murder.

"Aaahhhhh!"

***

"Aaahhhhh!" Shatira's screams ripped through the air, coming out of the kitchen's window and reaching Menace's bedroom window. The young nigga was fast asleep, but the shrilling awoke him from his slumber. His head snapped up from his pillow and he looked from left to right, wondering where the screaming was coming from. His chest jumped up and down. He was breathing hard, because that terrified shriek scared the hell out of him.

There was silence, but then, he heard the screaming again.

"Aaahhhhhhhh!"

"Shatira!" Menace's sleepy eyes came alive and he jumped out of bed, gold chain swinging from left to right. He still had on the clothes he'd worn out to the movies that night, so all he had to do was throw on some of his murder gear. He slipped on his Nike baseball gloves and hoodie, zipping it up to the top. He then tied a red bandana over the lower half of his face and threw the hood on his head, enclosing it around his head. Next, he lifted his mattress and grabbed his banga. He chambered a copper, bald head bullet into its head and tucked it on his waistline, as he headed out of his bedroom door.

When Menace reached the living room, he found Ducey, his father's best friend, drawing dope from a soggy piece of cotton that was in a spoon saturated by liquid heroin. Once the syringe was filled with dope, Ducey turned around to Fonzell, who he was sitting beside him on the couch. Fonzell, who was Menace's father, was looking down at a thick vein in his arm.

Fonzell was a high-yellow nigga with hazel green eyes. He had scruffy facial hair and reddish brown hair that was pushing the perm up from his roots. Fonzell looked exactly like Terrance Howard when he played Cowboy in *Dead Presidents*, except he was in his late thirties.

Back in the day, Fonzell was a struggling musician trying to be heard by anyone that would listen. He played in every hole-in-the-wall and two-bit nightclub that would have him. The pay was shitty, but he was given as many drinks and food as he desired. Although his aspirations weren't supporting him financially, he didn't give a fuck. People were feeling his music and he was garnering a buzz locally; that was all he cared about.

Unfortunately, Fonzell's musical dreams came to a tragic end on the day the hand he played his guitar with was severed. Sure, he could have went on to play with his other hand, but the murder of his son's mother, Moochie, shortly thereafter, extinguished his desire to sing and play the guitar completely. Fonzell found himself in a very dark place. He was depressed and suicidal, but he couldn't bring himself to take his own life knowing he had a son to raise. Unable to cope and with growing responsibilities to boot, Fonzell turned to heroin to escape the harsh realities of his life.

Fonzell's dealer then, Ducey, winded up becoming his best friend and running partner.

Homie had fucked around and tried his own dope to see why dope fiends loved some shit so much that destroyed their lives. His curiosity cost him his lavish lifestyle and countless friends and family. Since his addiction to dope, Ducey and Fonzell had been as thick as thieves, running the streets trying to gather every nickel and dime they could to get their next fix.

Menace had done everything in his power to get Fonzell help for his habit, but he refused to seek treatment. So he said fuck it, and left his fate in God's hands.

The Streets Don't Love Nobody

Menace watched his father and his homeboy for a moment before making a beeline for the front door shaking his head, shamefully. He had murder on his mind and a banga in the front of his Dickies. His gloved hand grasped the front door's knob. He was about to twist it and pull the door open, when the man who's nuts he was shot out of spoke up.

"You sure you wanna do it like that, son? You think she's worth it?" Fonzell asked him about Shatira. He knew his boy had a thing for the girl next door, but he didn't know how serious it was. At the time, Fonzell's head was laid back against the couch, as Ducey pushed the dope from out of the needle into his arm. As the heroin was released into his bloodstream, Ducey unstrapped the belt from around his partner's arm with his freehand.

At that moment, Menace's back was to Fonzell and Ducey and he was still holding the door knob. He gave his father's question some thought before looking over his shoulder to answer him.

"She's worth it and then some," Menace slipped out of the door and into the night.

Once Menace was gone, Ducey shook his head and said, "That knucklehead son of yours gon' fuck around and get himself killed behind some pussy."

"Like father like son," Fonzell said, slowly shutting his eyelids. He drifted off as the dope in his system began to work its magic.

***

"Get off me, get the fuck off meeeee!" Shatira shrilled at the top of her lungs with tears in her eyes. She was struggling to get up from the floor as Levon held her wrists down. The sick, perverted bastard tried to plant hickeys on her neck.

Boom!

The back door went flying open, sending a chunk of the door frame and splinters flying everywhere. Menace came running in, a pair of intimidating eyes peeking over a red bandana, a gloved hand gripping a fat ass gun.

"Don't move! Bet notta mothafucka in here move!" Menace waved his head bussa around daring anybody to act up, so he could give them some act-right. Everyone froze in terror. The sight of that pretty black thang put the fear God in them niggaz. Menace's eyes darted over to Levon, who was positioned between Shatira's thick legs, looking over his shoulders at him. Sweat was dripping from his brow having been struggling with Shatira for her innocence.

"Get the fuck offa me!" Shatira screamed and punched on him. Levon turned his head and threw up his arms to deflect her punches.

"Bitch ass nigga, you was finna rape my boo!" Menace snatched Levon off of Shatira and flipped his gun over in his hand, cracking old boy upside in the face with it. He then slammed him up against the refrigerator and jammed his weapon inside of his grill, puffing his jaws out.

"Arghhhh!" Levon's eyes bulged as he gagged on the gun, blood dripping from his bottom lip. While Menace was holding him up against the refrigerator, a sobbing Shatira got to her feet trying her best to cover up by pulling her torn shirt upon her breasts.

The Streets Don't Love Nobody

"I should peel yo' fuckin' onion nigga!" A scowling Menace's voice boomed, slightly muffled the bandana over the lower half of his face.

Seeing everyone distracted, Delores edged herself along the sink keeping her eyes on everything. Once she reached the knife block, she drew the butcher's knife.

Snikt!

Delores smiled fiendishly and licked her lips seeing Menace at her mercy. "Aaaaah!" she screamed like a mad woman as she charged forward, shoving Shatira out of her way and lifting the butcher's knife above her head.

Menace whipped around and kicke Delores hard as fuck in her stomach, doubling her over. She dropped the butcher's knife and he whacked her across the face with his banga, spilling her to the floor. kicking in her stomach so hard that her eyes bugged and she doubled over holding her sides. Hearing hurried footfalls at his left, Menace whipped around to find LaRon running at him, a meat cleaver held above his head, screaming at the top of his lungs.

Menace pointed his gun at that bitch ass nigga, stopping him dead in his tracks. "Drop that fucking cleaver and say, ah!" LaRon did what he was told and Menace shoved his banga inside of his mouth, causing him to gag on the end of it.

"You fucking asshole!" Shatira charged forward and cracked Levon in the jaw, whipping his head around. He slowly turned his head back around, smiling evilly at her with bloody teeth. Levon, the sick motahfucka that he was, licked the blood from off his teeth and swallowed that shit.

"Hahahahahahaha!" Levon laughed maniacally, staring into Shatira's eyes.

"Oh, you think that's funny, huh? Well, wait for the punchline!" Shatira hauled off and kicked him between the legs. Levon grabbed his aching balls as he bent at the waist, eyes looking like they were about to burst from their sockets. She followed up, kicking him in the jaw and spilling him to floor. He lay there bawling and holding his meat. Looking down up him, Shatira kicked him in the chest and spat on it.

"Tira, pack you some clothes and shit. I got conrol of shit down here." Menace orderd her, looking around at Levon and Delores. They were both still in pain.

"Okay," Shatira ran out of the kitchen. She came back less than five minutes with a small duffle bag.

"You got all you need, slim?" Menace inquired.

"Yeah," she nodded.

"Alright then. Let's go!" Menace smacked LaRon with his gun and he dopped to his hands and knees, spitting blood on the floor.

Menace tucked his gun at the small of his back. He then grabbed Shatira's hand and they fled out of the house. As soon as they'd left, Delores scrambled to her feet and went to retrieve her double barrel shotgun. A second later, she was sprinting across the kitchen floor, snapping the double pips of the powerful weapon closed.

***

Menace and Shatira ran out of the house, hand in hand. They could feel and hear Delores' wicked ass on their heels, talking big shit. Her evil aura was stronger than the stench of a rotten corpse. They glanced over their shoudlers, and sure enough, there she was with a fat ass shotgun.

"Mothafucka gon' come up in my house popping all of dat shit? I got something for yo' dog ass! Delores hoisted up the double barrel shotgun and Menace's eyes bulged.

"Oh, shit!" Menace hollered out, pulling Shatira low to the ground with him. The shotgun roared just as they ducked the fire from it.

Bloom!

The recoil of the shotgun caused Delores to stagger backwards and nearly fall. She was regaining her balance as Menace and Shatira were mounting a motorcycle. A man in a yellow motorcycle racing suit had just walked away from the bike, removing his helmet. At the moment, he was approaching a woman who was coming down the steps of a nearby house, with a glass bottle of Coca Cola. Luckily for Menace and Shatira, he'd left his keys in the sexy machine.

As soon as Menace and Shatira hopped upon the motorcycle. The woman with the Coca Cola pointed them out to the man in the racing suit. The man threw his helmet down to the lawn and went running towards Menace and Shatira.

"Hey, what the fuck are you doin'?" the man called out. When he looked to his right and saw Delores with that shotgun, he took off running in the opposite direction. He grabbed the hand of the woman with the Coca Cola and they ran inside of her house, slamming the door shut behind them.

"You done fucked up, nigga! Big Time!" Delores told Menace as she ran towards him and Shatira. She stopped and fired her shotgun, but missed them.

Tranay Adams

"Shit, shit, shit!" Menace cussed, as he was having trouble getting the motorcycle to start up. He gave it three tries, but the bastard still wouldn't start. Feeling Shatira smack him on his arm in a panic, he looked over his shoulder and saw Delores reloading her shotgun. This sped up his heart rate and he could feel the blood in his body, rushing throughout his veins. "Come on, baby, come on!" he talked to the motorcycle as if it was his girlfriend. "Work for daddy, I need you to come through for me, boo. Show yo' nigga some love."

"Oh, my God, Menace!" Shatira shouted, smacking his arm even harder. When Menace looked at his back, he saw that evil bitch Delores, clamping her double barrel shotgun shut.

"Come on baby," Menace caressed the handlebar of the bike, lovingly. It looked like he was caressing the cheek of the woman he was in love with. He stole another glance over his shoulder and saw Delores lifting her shotgun up to fire it. His head whipped back around and he tried the bike again. It cranked right up, then. Its headlight shined brightly, illuminating the street before him. He clicked up the kickstand with the heel of his sneaker and twisted the rubber grips back and forth, revving the beast up.

Vroom! Vrooom! Vroooom!

Smoke spat out of the chrome exhausted pipes and he mashed the pedals. The motorcycle flew down the block, with its riders ducking their heads as a thunderous clap erupted in the night.

"Goddamn it!"Delores shouted, hating she'd missed the chance to blow Menace and Shatira's heads off. She ran out into the middle of the street and lifted the twin barrels.

The Streets Don't Love Nobody

Bloom!

Smoke and sparks rolled out of the twin pipes, but the weapon wasn't any threat from the distance it was fired from.

"We clear?" Menace shouted over his shoulder to Shatira, without turning around.

She turned her head back around from looking at her stepmother, who was standing out in the street, hurling threats and waving her shotgun. Levon and LaRon had just run out into the street with their guns.

"We're clear!"Shatira told him, lying her head against his back and wrapping her arms around his waist. Closing her eyes, she knew that she was in love with him because she'd never felt as safe with anyone in her life as she did in that moment. Menace's eyes darted to their left, feeling Shatira cozy up to him. It was from this, that he could tell she was comfortable with him and he liked that.

A Smirk curled the end of Menace's lips and he mashed the gas pedal further, causing the motorcycle to rip up the block with an angry squeal.

***

Fonzell grunted as he pumped between her legs, beads of sweat rolling down his body and arms. Droplets of sweat fell from his brow and splashed on her ample bosoms.

"Ah, shit! Ah, fuck, yo' pussy good, it's real good!" Fonzell's face was balled up and his jaws were locked, displaying his teeth.

"Uh! Uh! Uh! Uh!" Moochie cried out as his dick moved in and out of her pussy. Her hair was a mess and she was also covered in sweat.

"I'm finna cum, baby. I'm finna cum in this pussy," he announced to her.

"Cum, daddy, cum in my pussy. Fill it up, fill it all the way up!" she whined, as she clawed at his back, breaking the skin and leaving red streaks behind.

Fonzell fucked her harder and faster, and before he knew it, he was spilling his warm seeds deep inside of her womb. Even after he had relieved himself, he continued to pump inside of her.

Exhausted, Fonzell collapsed on the side of her and she placed the side of her face on his chest. She stared out at nothing as she caressed his stomach. He lay on his back with his fingers interlocked behind his head, staring up at the ceiling. The only thing that could be heard were the lovers' labored breathing, as the smell of hot, sweaty sex lingered the bedroom.

"We fucked up. We really, really fucked up," Moochie stated, regretting to have cheated on her husband.

"I know, but fuck it." Fonzell replied.

She looked up at him from where she lay with her head against his chest. "Why you say fuck it?"

"It is what it is, Moochie," he told her. "You're a good woman. Any nigga out here would kill to have you, and here this mothafucka is beating on you like you ain't shit? What kinda man does that to a woman he claims to love, huh? What kind of man?" he inquired as he stared into her eyes, *caressing the side of her face. "I'll tell you what kind of man, a cowardly one."*

"You know if he ever found out about us, he'd have both of us killed, right? Where ever he found us, he'd kill us both dead. On the spot! No talking, or nothing. Just boom!" she made her hand into the shape of a gun and pretended to shoot him.

"Yeah, I know, but I ain't scared of him. As a matter of fact, I'm not scared of nothing in this world, just as long as I have you by my side."

She smiled and said, "Oh, really?"

"Fa sho'." he kissed her tenderly.

"That was nice."

"Real nice."

"Promise me something, okay?" Moochie said, staring him square in his eyes.

"Anything, beautiful." Fonzell told her as he played in her hair.

"Should he ever find out about us, you'll protect me, right?"

"That goes without saying, you know I got cho back."

Fonzell and Moochie kissed passionately. Then they made love again for the second time that night.

Ducey sat on the opposite end of the couch, pulling his belt tight around his arm. Once he'd buckled the belt, he smacked his track marked arm until a vein appeared. He took the syringe from out of his mouth and was about to shoot up, when he looked to Fonzell. Fonzell was slumped on the couch, with his right sleeve rolled up. The arm with the sleeve rolled up was the same one that Ducey had given him the shot of dope in.

Fonzell's eyelids were shut and a smile was spread across his face. The dope had taken him back to a happier time he'd shared with his deceased lover, Moochie Brown. Their love was forbidden, but that didn't stop them from experiencing one another. At the time, them being together was so wrong, but it felt so right.

"That goes without saying; you know I got cho back," Fonzell said, as he believed he was in that moment so many years ago that he was recalling. The smile on his face slowly turned upside down. Sadness spread across his face as his bottom lip quivered. Tears burst from his eyes and slid down his cheeks. "You know I got cho back..." he whimpered. "Oh, God, I'm sorry, baby. I'm so sorry; I couldn't protect you from 'em. Please, forgive me, baby. Please, forgive me." Fonzell peeled his eyelids open and sat up, placing his hand against his face. His shoulders shuddered as he broke down sobbing louder and louder.

Seeing his homeboy grieving, Ducey removed the belt from around his arm and sat it on the arm of the couch. He then capped the syringe and sat it down on the coffee table. Next, he scooted over to Fonzell and comforted him as best as he could, gripping his shoulder. He told him that everything was going to be alright, but truthfully, he didn't believe the shit himself. You see, he knew that Fonzell wouldn't ever get over the death of Moochie. He'd been grieving her death for as long as he could remember, and shit seemed to be getting worse and worse for him with each day that past. The only

The Streets Don't Love Nobody

thing that kept him going was the love of his son and his love of good dope. Those were two things that he couldn't see himself leaving behind in his death.

Suddenly, Fonzell stopped sobbing and took a deep breath. He wiped his crying eyes with the back of his stump and looked to Ducey. His eyes were pink and glassy. Homie looked like he had been smoking weed.

"My bad, Ducey, I'm over here crying and shit, like a lil' ol' bitch," Fonzell sniffled and wiped his eyes again.

"It's all good, bruh. I know how it is, shit's rough," Ducey told him, lifting his blue apple jack from off his head and scratching his brow. He then sat the cap back on his head. "Luckily, the Lord made this shit here," he held up the syringe, "So niggaz like you and I can escape our troubles, you feel what I'm saying?"

"Yeaaah," he smiled and nodded. "God bless good dope."

"Now, I'd like to get high, do you mind?" he passed him the syringe, suggesting that he shoot it into his arm for him. Next, he gave him the belt so he could tighten it around his arm.

"I got chu faded." Fonzell bit down on the syringe and pulled the belt tight around Ducey's arm, buckling it. Once he found a vein in his running partner's arm, he shot him with the dope, and watched as it took its effects.

Once Fonzell seen that his man was straight, he headed into the bathroom and shut the door behind him. He turned on the faucet and the shower water which quickly flooded the room with a humid fog. Afterwards, he balled up into a fetal position on the floor and cried his eyes out, thinking about his long, lost love, Moochie.

Chapter Seven

After blasting at Menace and Shatira, Delores switched hands with her double barrel shotgun and headed back toward her house. Levon and LaRon followed her back inside of the house and shut the door, locking it behind them.

"We needa hide these guns. I know the police are on their way with all of that gunfire." Delores said to the twins and passed LaRon her shotgun. She then took Levon's gun and handed it to him as well. "Baby boy, I want chu to wipe those guns down and stash them inside of the attic."

"I'm on it, ma," LaRon assured her. He switched hands with her shotgun and tucked Levon's gun into his waistline.

"That's my baby." Delores smiled as she looked into her son's eyes, caressing the side of his face. LaRon smirked and headed up the staircase to do like his mother had instructed. Once he was gone, she headed into the bathroom to scrub the gunpowder residue from off her hands in case the police came to their door.

"Momma, what chu want me to do?" Levon asked his mother as he followed her through the hallway.

Delores stopped and turned around to her oldest boy. Holding him by his chin, she turned his face from side to side, taking a good look at him.

"That punk ass nigga done ruined my baby's handsome face," she frowned as she took stock of Levon's injuries. The right side of his face was black and blue from Menace pistol whipping him. On top of that, his lips were busted and his front tooth was chipped the young nigga shoving his banga inside of his mouth. "Nah, I don't have anything I want chu to do. I'ma take care of your wounds once I finish scrubbing this gunpowder from off my hands. Meet me in my room; I'll be there in a bit with the first-aid kit." She started to head to the bathroom, but he called after her again, prompting her to turn around.

"Homeboy that busted in here tonight," Levon said, holding a mad dog stare.

"What about him, son?" Delores inquired as her brows wrinkled curiously. Her hands were on her hips and she was looking up at him.

"I know who he is. He and his dope fiend father live next door to us." He told her. "The streets call 'em Menace. As a matter of fact, I seen 'em walking with Shatira and her homegirl earlier today."

"Oh, really?" she said, lifting her eyebrow.

"Yeah," Levon nodded.

Hearing footsteps behind him, Levon looked over his shoulder and found LaRon approaching. His younger brother came to stand beside him in the corridor.

"What y'all talking about?" LaRon asked as his forehead crinkled.

"That nigga that ran off with Shatira is Menace," Levon reported.

"For real?" LaRon's eyes widen with surprise.

Levon nodded and looked back to his mother. "Look, ma, lemmie and baby bruh grab them thangs and go over there and smoke that nigga'z old man. Let 'em know, he put his hands on the wrong mothafucking family. You know what I'm saying?" Levon rubbed his hands together evilly. From the look on his face his mother could tell that her son wanted to get into some shit.

"Shiiiit, I'm always up for some gunplay," LaRon rubbed his hands together evilly, looking exactly like his twin brother.

"Whadda ya say, ma?" Levon asked, hoping his mother would give him the word to blow Fonzell's brains out.

"Hmmmm," Delores said as she turned her back on the twins, massaging her chin and giving it some thought. Having come to her conclusion, she turned back around to her boys. "You boys are gonna have to let this one ride until further notice. If you go smoke that hype next door, within next couple of days, I'm sure the police will put two and two together. Then, they'll come knocking at our door. We wouldn't want any blowback from the murder, so let's play it cool for a while, then we'll get some get-back. How does that sound?" she looked between her two boys, waiting to hear what they had to say.

Levon and LaRon exchanged glances and nodded at their mother.

"Alright then, that settles it. Y'all give ya momma some love," she opened her arms and her sons embraced her, kissing her on either side of her face.

Forty five minutes later

Menace and Shatira ended up at the Snooty Foxx off Manchester. After paying for their room, Menace led Shatira upstairs to their unit. When he opened the door and flipped on the light switch, he took a good look at the place they'd be staying at sfor a while. It was modestly furnished. There was a queen sized bed, a nightstand that had a lamp and personalized Bible on it, and a small round table and chair beside the window. Menace closed the door shut. He then removed his gold chain and put it into the nightstand's drawer. Next, he removed his hoodie and placed it on the back of the chair. When Menace turned around, he found Shatira sitting down on the bed beside her duffle bag, taking in the furnishings of the room like he had been. Suddenly, her face twitched and trembled, her eyes misted with tears. She whimpered and smacked her hands over her face, body rocking as she sobbed.

"Ah! Ha! Ha! Ha! Ha!" Shatira's head bobbed as she cried and leaned forward, with her elbows on her knees.

Menace's brows wrinkled seeing the pretty young girl crying her eyes out. After whipping out his banga, he sat it down on the nightstand and approached Shatira. He sat down beside her. He went to lift his arm to comfort her, but before he could she threw herself into him. She wrapped her arms around him and buried her face into his shirt, crying her eyes out.

"Shhhhhh, it's okay, ma, everything is gonna be alright." Menace tried his best to console her, stroking her back, soothingly. "What you went through was traumatic. It was very traumatic. Them mothafucking punk ass twins disrespected you, but I promise you one thang, they asses is gon' pay with their lives for what they did to you."

Shatira stopped crying, and pulled her face away from Menace's shirt, looking up into his face. Her eyes were pink and her cheeks were soaked. She sniffled and said, "Put that on yo' hood you gon' kill them punk ass niggaz...Delores bitch ass, too."

The Streets Don't Love Nobody

Menace looked her square in her eyes, with seriousness bleeding from them. "I put that on Eastside Outlaw Twenties, I'ma smoke that whole mothafucking family. Word is bond!" he tapped the Blood gang sign against his chest to emphasize exactly what he was saying. There was nothing more sacred to him than his dead mother's name and his hood.

She nodded and said, "I believe you."

"You betta, 'cause nothing is more important to me than my honor."

Menace held out his fist, signaling to her to dap him up. She smirked and obliged him. He returned the gesture and gave her a loving hug. Right then, his cellular rang and vibrated inside of his pocket. He pulled it out and looked at the display. It was his father so he answered it. Through hand gestures, Shatira communicated to him that she was going to take a shower and he nodded. With that understanding, she grabbed her duffle bag from off the bed and went to take care of her hygiene.

"What's up, pop?" Menace said as soon as he placed the cell phone to his ear. His old man was asking him about the gunfire he heard outside. Menace went on to tell him what had occurred and where he'd be laying his head at that night. "Yeah, pop, we straight, but you know how I do. I may need you with me when I take care of that business, too. Yep, love you too, OG."

Menace disconnected the call. Once the screen of the timer of the call disappeared, he was left with an old picture of his mother, Moochie, which was his screen saver. He smiled as he stared down at the picture of his mother on his device's display. Slowly, his eyes became glassy and the smile vanished from his lips.

"You were so beautiful, momma. You were hands down, the most beautiful woman in the whole wide world." Menace professed, as his eyes filled with tears and spilled down his cheeks. The young nigga sniffled and licked his lips, continuing his admiring of the woman that had given birth to him in the picture. "I swear to God, ma. I'd do any and everything to have you here with me right now. Life can be so unfair; I didn't even get a chance to really get to know you like that. Damn." he bowed his head and shook it. When he looked back up, big teardrops fell from the brims of his eyelids and splashed on the picture that he was holding.

"Babe, are you, okay?" Shatira asked as she emerged from out of the bathroom. Menace was startled when he saw her. He'd been so engrossed in the picture of his deceased mother on his cell phone that he hadn't heard her return to the room.

"Yeah, yeah, I'm good, slim," Menace said, wiping his dripping eyes as fast as he could. He didn't want Shatira to see him crying. Rising from off the bed, he moved to put his cell phone away, but she engaged him. She plucked the picture from his pinched fingers and looked at it.

"My God, she's beautiful. Probably the most beautiful woman I've ever seen in my life." Shatira said, truly amazed by Menace's mother's stunning good looks. "Who is she? Your aunt? Your mother?"

"My mom," Menace nodded. He then took his cellular from her and sat it down on the nightstand, beside the lamp.

"Right. I remember you saying your mom died some time ago." she said, climbing into bed and lying across it. "How'd she die?"

The Streets Don't Love Nobody

Menace took off his chain and laid it upon the nightstand. He then sat back down on the bed, kicking off his sneakers and removing his socks. He turned toward Shatira and took a breath. He ran his hands down his face, before going on to tell the story.

Moochie stood on the side of a liquor store wearing an oversized hoodie. She carefully peeked around the corner of the establishment to see a D-boy in a doo-rag and baggy jeans. The youngsta looked up and down the block for any night stalkers looking to cop their poison of choice. A minute later, a scraggly looking dope fiend ambled over to him, scratching his scabbed arm. Seeing the bleeding from the junkie's fingernails raking up against the scabs caused the D-boy to cringe.

"Lemmie get two," the dope fiend held up two ashy fingers, which had blood and dirt caked up under their fingernails.

The D-boy checked his surroundings to make sure the coast was clear, while he pulled out to packets of dope from his rather deep pocket. He swapped the drugs for the crumbled up five dollar bills the hype had in his possession. As soon as the exchange was made, the fiend darted off into the opposite direction, where he was swallowed up by the darkness of the night. Once he was gone, the D-boy stashed his profit into his pocket and continued to watch the streets he was pedaling dope on.

Having seen the exchange, Moochie pulled her head back around the corner and pulled the T-shirt she was wearing around her neck over the lower half of her face. She then pulled out an old, beat-up Colt .45, with dirty tape around its handle. The damn thing only had two bullets in it, and she was hoping she wouldn't have to use them, but if it

*came down to it, she was sure she wouldn't hesitate to bust a
cap in a nigga'z ass.*

*Moochie leaned her head back against the building
and shut her eyelids, bringing her revolver up to her shoulder.
She took a few breaths, which ruffled the shirt she was
wearing over her mouth.*

*"Come on, girl, you gotta do this shit. You need this
fix, you all sick and shit out here." Moochie brought her head
back down and glanced around the corner again. She spotted
the D-boy serving another dope fiend, that had just so
happened to be walking away. Moochie pulled her head back
around the corner, swallowed the lump of fear in her throat,
and gripped her pistol tighter. "Fuck it! I'm on this nigga'z
ass!"*

*Moochie swung from around the corner of the liquor
store, Colt up and pointed at the D-boy. He had just turned
from looking up the block and met the hollow barrel of her
revolver. Instantly, the D-boy's eyes doubled in size and his
mouth opened, displaying his chipped front tooth. He started
to run, but thought better of it when Moochie shouted a
warning.*

*"Unh, unh, don't even move, mothafucka, or I swear
before God and Heaven, I'ma leave yo' black ass on the same
corner you slangin' yo dope on! Put cho hands up, put cho
gotdamn hands up, now!" Moochie commanded.*

*"Yo', ma, what the fuck you want?" the D-boy asked
as he held his hands up. Moochie looked him dead in his eyes
and pressed the cold barrel of the Colt against the side of his
nose.*

The Streets Don't Love Nobody

"Every-mothafucking-thang!" she told him with a pair of cold eyes. Still holding her .45 to the side of homeboy's snout, Moochie went about the task of relieving him of all the dope he had on him. Once she pocketed the drugs, she searched his pockets for any money he may have on him.

While Moochie was going through the D-boy's pockets, he focused his attention on the chamber of the revolver. He noticed that it was only loaded with two copper, bald head bullets, but they were two trigger squeezes away from the weapon's barrel. With that in mind, the D-boy decided to take a chance.

"Jackpot," Moochie smiled behind the shirt tied around the lower half of her face. She'd just pulled a handful of wrinkled bills from her victim's pocket. Suddenly, her eyes grew as big as saucers when she felt the D-boy grabbed hold of her pistol with both hands. She dropped the money she'd just pulled out of his pocket and grabbed hold of her weapon, with her other hand. She and homeboy grunted as they fought for control of the revolver, both knowing that possession of it meant life or death.

"You fuckin' bitch, tryna rob me for my mothafucking paypa? On God, I'ma kill yo' punk ass out here on this corna!" the D-boy swore through gritted teeth, as the barrel of the .45 neared Moochie's face. Her forehead was sweaty due to the struggle she'd put up against homeboy for the control of the Colt. And now, the deadly end of the pistol was an inch away from her face. Although she was putting up one hell of a fight, her efforts weren't any match for the strength of a grown-ass man.

"Aaaaaahh!" Moochie hollered out, fearful of being shot. She could see down the pitch-black barrel of the Colt .45. It clicked twice as its trigger was pulled twice. Right then,

she knew without a shadow of a doubt that death lurked inside of the revolver.

Blam!

Fire ripped past Moochie's head, missing her by half an inch. She kneed the D-boy in the balls and his eyes bulged. He dropped down to his knees, holding his crotch with one hand and the Colt .45 in the other. Down on his knees on the sidewalk, the D-boy coughed and winced, feeling as if his nuts were inside of his stomach. When he looked up, he saw Moochie rounding the corner of the liquor store as she ran for her life.

Blam!

A bullet broke off the edge of the brick building, sending debris flying. The slug had barely missed Moochie, so he kept on pulling the trigger, back to back. The chamber of the revolver twisted and clicked empty, each time. Realizing that the pistol was empty, the D-boy tossed the piece aside and scrambled to his feet. He pulled his Glock from the small of his back and limped after Moochie. He found her back as he rounded the corner of the liquor store. Angry and in pain, he pointed the banga and squeezed off.

Blocka! Blocka! Blocka!

Moochie screamed in a panic as she darted across the intersection, head ducked down. She was running so fast that she looked like a blur to homeboy that was busting at her ass.

Suddenly, a van slammed into Moochie, sending her body flying upon its windshield and then crashing to the ground. She lay in the middle of the street awkwardly, lying deathly still. The D-boy lowered his banga to his side and looked around as he speed walked toward Moochie, moving with a limp. Once he reached her, he switched hands with his Glock and pulled her over on her back. She was looking out at the world through vacant eyes. There was blood running out of her left nostril and both of her ears. Moochie was dead.

"Say, brotha, is she okay?" A voice inquired from over the D-boy's shoulder. When the D-boy looked, he saw a tall, scrawny white dude with long blonde hair and a beard the hid most of his face. He was in a small white T-shirt and overalls.

The D-boy held his head down and threw his arm up to shield his face. He didn't want anyone to identify him and connect him to Moochie's untimely death. He sprinted back toward the way he came, and disappeared down a dark alley.

"Awww, shit, she'd dead!" the driver of the van announced, having just check Moochie's pulse. His eyes lingered on her dead body for a while longer, before he jogged across the street to a pay phone. After he snatched the telephone from off its hook, he dialed 9-1-1 and waited for someone to answer. While he waited, he looked back and forth between the telephone booth and Moochie's lifeless body, like he expected her to rise from the dead or shit. But that wasn't happening, homegirl was long gone. "Hello! This black lady ran out into the middle of the street and I winded up hitting her. Yeah, I checked her pulse, I believe she's dead."

Having heard the story, Shatira crawled over to Menace and wrapped her arms around his neck, resting her chin on his shoulder.

"I'm sorry about what happened to your mother, I really am," Shatira said, misty eyed, "I lost both of my parents, and I can tell you, although you never get over it, the pain lessens with every day that passes. It never goes away, but it makes it a little easier to deal with."

I know," a glassy eyed Menace patted her on the arm and presented her with a weak smile. "Lemmie get up and wash my ass 'fore I lay down."

"Okay," she replied, placing her forehead to the back of his for a moment, and then kissing it. She lay back down on the bed and turned on the television with the remote.

Menace rose from off the bed and headed to the bathroom, unbuckling his belt. He entered the bathroom, turning on the light and shutting the door behind him.

Twenty-five minutes later

Shatira lay on her side in bed staring at the bathroom door. The lights were out, but the light from inside of the bathroom outlined the door's frame, highlighting it. The bathroom door opened and Menace walked out, clad in boxer shorts. Shatira took in his frame which was ripped with muscles. She could tell that the young gangsta worked out regularly, his well defined form was proof of this. Little momma couldn't tell that he was buff underneath his clothes, so she was quite surprised.

Shatira was getting hot and bothered, squeezing her thighs together. Menace's muscular body and his tattoos gave him mad sex appeal. The ink on his body made him look like a real thug ass nigga. He had Easty above his right brow, Outlaw 20s on his neck, a crucifix on his back in honor of his deceased mother, RTB on his right peck, his mother's face on his left peck and South Central across his stomach. These were just some of the tattoos that attributed to the artwork covering his body.

The Streets Don't Love Nobody

Menace walked over to the bed, grabbing a pillow and a sheet. Shatira rose up in bed and looked at Menace, brows wrinkled.

"Where are you going?" Shatira inquired.

"You ain't know? I'ma gangsta and a gentleman. I'ma let chu have the bed, I'll take the floor." Menace smirked, tossing his pillow down on the floor at the foot of the bed. He then draped his sheet on the floor, and then his blanket. He was about to lay down, when he saw the perplexed look on Shatira's face.

"What's up, slim?" he asked.

"Oh...nothing." she shook her head, fluffing her pillow and laying her head against it.

"You sure?"

Without looking at him, Shatira held her hand into the air and gave him a thumb up. Menace shrugged and lay down on the floor, placing his hands behind his head as he stared at the ceiling.

Shatira's thoughts were plagued with sexual thoughts of Menace as she lay in bed. With her eyelids closed, she watched herself have sex with him. Seeing the movie playing behind her eyelids, she found her pussy growing wet. Before she knew it, her nipples stiffened. She licked her bottom lip and bit down on it. She then slipped her hands under her shirt and fondled her breasts. Her hips started moving like she was riding a dick, as she dipped one of her hands inside of her panties, playing with her clit. Her masturbating got so good to her that her face contorted into a mask of pleasure. She threw her head back and her mouth quivered. The movements of her hips sped up, and she gasped. She found herself panting as she neared an orgasm.

"Uh!" Shatira's eyelids snapped open and she smacked her hand over her mouth. She didn't mean to get so loud while pleasuring herself. She hoped that Menace didn't hear her. Easing up from off the bed, she tried to peek over the edge of the bed to see if Menace was still up, but she couldn't see him. "Uh, um, Menace?"

"What's up?" Menace answered.

'Fuck' Shatira mouthed to herself, hating that Menace was still up. She was positive he'd heard her now. Saying fuck it, she decided to call him upon the bed.

"What's up, lil' momma? What's wrong?" Menace laid his arm across the edge of the bed and looked over at Shatira, wondering what was on her mind.

"Ummm, I'm still a little shaken up by what occurred back at my house. Do you mind sleeping up here in the bed with me?" she asked him with a pleading look in her eyes.

"Fa sho'."

Menace snatched up his pillow, tossing it onto the bed beside Shatira and climbed into it. He lay on his side so he'd be facing Shatira's back and shut his eyelids. Shatira frowned up noticing that she didn't feel Menace up against her. She looked over her shoulder and found him on his side of the bed. She lay her head back down, shut her eyelids and took a breath. In doing this, she was mustering up the courage to ask him for what she really wanted.

"Um, Menace?" she called out to him.

The Streets Don't Love Nobody

"'Sup, ma?" he peeled his eyelids open.

"You mind holding me in your arms. I mean, if it's not too much trouble," she looked over at him, hoping he'd say yes. She'd die if he told her no, but something told her that he'd grant her request.

"No problem." Menace brought his pillow closer to Shatira and scooted over to her. He threw his arm over her, and she scooted her ass up against him. A smile stretched across her face as she shut her eyelids, pulling his arm tighter around her. It felt good to her to be in the strong embrace of a man that was willing to kill to protect her. She hadn't felt this safe since her father had died, and she never wanted the feeling to go away...ever.

Menace shut his eyelids and bowed his forehead against the back of Shatira's head, inhaling the enticing scent from her shampooed hair. "Mmmm, you smell good. What chu put in your hair?"

"This leave in African conditioner called Cantu. I started buying a while ago. You like it?"

"I love it."

"Thank you," the right side of her mouth curled with a grin.

Silence impregnated the bedroom. The youngstas lay in bed in the comfort of one another, eyelids shut, mouths closed. Suddenly, Shatira's eyelids peeled open, and she smirked. Feeling Menace's hardness pressed against her ass, she couldn't help wondering what was on his mind.

"Uh, Menace?" she called him in a sweet, sultry voice.

"Yeah?"

"Um, uh, what is that pressed against my booty?" she smiled.

Menace frowned as he didn't know what the hell she was talking about. It wasn't until he looked down and saw his rock hard dick lying firmly against her buttocks that he understood what she was getting at.

"Oh, shit, my bad!" he went to scoot back from her, but she grabbed his hand and insisted he stayed put. She then turned around to face him, meeting the surprised expression on his face. She cupped his face and stared into his eyes, smiling. He smiled back, enjoying her soft touch. He brought his hand up and caressed her cheek.

"Can I tell you a secret?" Shatira asked Menace.

"If you want too," Menace answered.

Shatira leaned closer to Menace and whispered, "I've been in love with you since the first time I saw you. I just never had the heart to tell you face to face."

"For real?" he asked, blushing hard as a mothafucka.

She smiled harder, seeing him blushing red. "Ooooh, look at chu. I didn't know gangstas blushed."

"Shut up, 'fore I kick yo' lil' ass out this bed," he said playfully, smiling.

Shatira chuckled and quieted down. She and Menace stared into one another's eyes, silently.

Menace cleared his throat and began, "Can I tell you a secret?"

The Streets Don't Love Nobody

"Uhn, huh," a smiling Shatira nodded.

"Well, I've been in love with chu since the first time I saw you, too. I just never knew how to come at chu with it. I mean, I was afraid that if I got at chu, that you may shoot me down."

"Really?" she looked at him disbelievingly.

"Yeah," he looked down, feeling ashamed.

"Wow! I'm in complete shock."

"Why's that?" he asked intrigued.

"Well, you're a hardcore gangbanger," she told him. "I thought you'd be more afraid of literally getting shot down in a drive by, then getting proverbially shot down by little old me."

"I Griff you. A nigga ain't afraid of nothing in this world, besides love."

She frowned and angled her head slightly, saying, "Love? Why are you afraid of love?" she wondered.

Menace took a deep breath, like it was going to be hard for him to tell her exactly what his reason was, before replying, "I lost my mom when I was two-years-old. She was the love of my pop life. He said he never loved any woman as much as he loved her. After her death, for as long as I can remember, my pop would cry every night. The loss of my mother hurt my OG so bad, that he turned to shooting dope, just to cope. I know if it wasn't for me, he would have killed himself a long time ago." his eyes turned glassy, and he looked like he was on the verge of crying. But the gangsta in him wouldn't allow the tears to fall. "He's never gotten over my mom's death. 'Til this day, when I look into my old head's eyes, I can see all the pain in them. So, when I think about what he embodies, I gotta tell you, if love gon' make a young nigga feel like that, then it's something I don't ever wanna experience. But I guess my heart has betrayed me, 'cause now it's too late."

Shatira's eyes grew watery, but she fought back the tears. She then cupped Menace's face again, kissing him on the forehead and saying, "With love, it's a damned if you do, damned if you don't kind of thing. It's like, if you don't let yourself go, and allow yourself to fall for an individual, then you're gonna miss out on one of the most beautiful experiences life has to offer you. And although it may be risky, it's definitely worth it."

"Yeah, it's most def' a risk," Menace agreed. "'Cause if you love someone, then your being vulnerable to 'em. You giving another human being this great power over you. They'll possess the power to hurt chu. And for a nigga like me, that's scary. I mean, really scary."

"I know, baby," she began, looking him square in the eyes. "But like you said, 'it's too late'. We already have those kinds of feelings for one another, so that means we already hold that power over each other's hearts. I tell you what, though. I'll vow not to ever abuse that power, if you vow to do the same."

"Okay. I vow not to abuse the power I have over you."

"I also vow not to abuse the power I have over you."

"Pinky swear?" Menace said seriously, holding up his curled pinky finger.

Shatira smirked and said, "Pinky swear."

The Streets Don't Love Nobody

Shatira and Menace hooked their pinky fingers. They then sealed the deal with a kiss. She held his hip while he cupped her face with his hand, kissing her slow and passionately. Their kissing sped up and their breathing grew heavier. They turned their heads in opposite directions as they made out, 'Mmmmmm's' escaped from their lips.

Menace broke away from Shatira's kiss. Dipping low, he kissed on her neck, and then sucked the soft flesh beneath her chin. As he was doing this, he slipped his hands underneath her shirt and groped her full, succulent breasts. Feeling his touch caused Shatira to mash her head back into the pillow. Her eyelids fluttered as she licked her lips. Menace lifted Shatira's shirt higher, and held a tittie in each hand. As he admired her ample breasts, he licked his lips, then feasted his eyes on her long, rigid nipples. Menace licked around the areolas of each tit, and flicked their nipples with the tip of his tongue. He then latched his mouth onto one breast at a time, sucking on them thirstily. Shatira gasped and pulled at the sheets, balling them into her fists. The sensation of Menace pleasuring her was driving her insane. Once he mashed her titties together, and sucked on both nipples at once, Shatira's eyes rolled to their whites.

"Oooooh, shiiit, woooo," Shatira winced. Her mouth trembled and stretched wide open. Right after, her pussy walls flooded with wetness. "Can I-can I touch it, baby?" she asked, looking down at Menace's concentrated face. His eyelids were narrowed into slits, and he looked focused on what he was trying to accomplish, which was making her orgasm.

"Touch what?" Menace posed a question of his own, as he continued to suck on her tits.

"Your-your dick...please."

With that having been asked, Menace stood up on his knees and pulled his underwear below his dick. Shatira sat up on her elbows and feasted her eyes on his hard-on. There his dick stood in all of its heavenly glory. It was fairly long, fat, and rippled with veins.

"I thought chu said you wanted to touch it." Menace said.

"I do," Shatira smiled.

"Well?" the corner of Menace's mouth curled and he hunched his shoulders, wondering when she was going to touch his steel pole.

Shatira grasped Menace's dick, slowly stroking it up and down. Hearing Menace grunting, she looked up and saw a blissful expression across his face. He licked his lips and bit down on his bottom one, appearing to be enjoying her stroking his dick. Shatira continued to stroke his shit up and down, faster. It turned her on hearing his masculine grunting, and knowing she was pleasing him. Her eyes dropped to his peel hole, and she saw pre-cum oozing out of it. Using her thumb, she rubbed his warm semen around the head of his thickness. She then continued to stroke him.

"Fuck, Blood, this shit feel good," he claimed, eyelids shut and head tilted back.

Shatira was delighted to hear his pleasure filled moans. His sensual sounds made her wetter. Without her realizing it, Shatira's hand dipped inside of her panties and she started fingering her clit. Her eyelids fluttered and she licked her lips, tilting her head back. She moaned in ecstasy, as she masturbated and gave her lover a hand-job.

The Streets Don't Love Nobody

"Do me a favor, baby," Menace's voice broke her concentration from her fingering herself. She looked up at him, waiting for him to tell her what was on his mind. "Hold 'em with both hands so I fuck yo' grip." He commanded, referring to his dick.

Shatira took Menace's dick into both of her hands. He held her shoulders as he began to thrust into her grip. She watched as the head of his member disappeared and reappeared between her hands. He'd started off slow at first, but then he began to speed up. Before she knew it, he was pumping feverishly, and groaning. Veins bulged in his forehead and arms. His eyelids were squeezed shut and his jaws were clenched tight. Menace gripped Shatira's shoulders tighter. The muscles in his back flexed as he continued to fuck his lover's grip.

Shatira started moaning. The look on Menace's face, coupled with his lustful stroking turned her on. She found herself growing hot and bothered. At that moment, she squeezed her thighs together, wanting to feel his fat ass dick in her pussy.

"You gon' cum for me, baby? Huh?" Shatira looked up at Menace, as he kept humping her grasp. By this time, his peel hole had leaked a clear fluid over her hands. He was super aroused then. His eyelids peeled open and he looked down at her, nodding yes. Having gotten the confirmation, Shatira placed her mouth over both her hands. She looked up at him, as his dick thrust passed the hole her hands formed and slid inside of her warm, wet mouth. Menace's face balled up. He licked his bottom lip and went faster. His speeding up caused her upper body to rock back and forth. She could tell by his movements he was nearing his nut, especially since he started moaning louder and louder.

Menace stopped humping Shatira's grip. Stroking his dick, he looked down at her and said, "I don't wanna bust yet, ma. I want some pussy."

Menace gently pushed Shatira back on the bed. He then slipped off her panties and lay them aside. Once he parted her legs, he stared down at her pussy. It was shaved and meaty. The most beautiful pussy he'd ever seen, hands down. Menace slid the shaft of his dick up and down Shatira's clit, causing her to gasp and squirm. He knew he was driving her crazy, and she was craving to have him stuffed between her legs, and that fed his ego, tremendously.

Menace tapped his dick against Shatira's clit. He then placed the tip of himself at the opening of her pussy, making the head of his member disappear. Menace bit down on his bottom lip in anticipation of feeling Shatira's drenched walls. He was just about to push himself inside of her when she spoke up.

"Baby, wait…" Shatira said, looking up at him. He was hunched over her and holding her legs apart.

"What's wrong?" Menace asked as a crease formed on his forehead.

"I'm not ready, yet. I'm sorry," she broke the news to him. From the look on her face he could tell that she was nervous about what he would say.

Damn, I hope he doesn't trip. I really am feeling him, and want to give myself to him. But I want to wait until the time is right. I hope he understands.

"Alright," Menace replied, releasing her legs and putting away his semi-erect dick. His shit sloped as soon as he heard he wasn't getting any pussy. He then grabbed his pillow and rose from the bed.

Seeing Menace rising to leave, Shatira slipped her panties back on and called out to him. "Wait, where you going?"

"Finna lay down."

"So, you don't wanna lay with me 'cause I'm not tryna give you no ass?" her forehead deepened with a line.

"Nah, it ain't even like that. A nigga ain't wetting it," he assured her. "I just thought that chu would wanna sleep alone. I mean, obviously something is bothering you, right? A nigga like me likes to be alone when he gotta lotta shit on his mind. You Griff me?"

Shatira nodded, and said, "It's nothing that's really bothering me, seriously. It's just that...it's just that. Well," she dropped her head, contemplating on whether she should tell him why she didn't want to have sex with him yet. If she laid the truth on him he could give her the deuces and bounce on her. That was the last thing she wanted to happen.

Seeing that Shatira had something on her mind, Menace tossed his pillow back on the bed. He then sat down and turned to her, brows furrowed with concern. He placed his hand on her thigh and caressed it, soothingly.

"What's the matter, slim? Holla at cho nigga. Lemmie know what's on yo' mind," he told her.

Shatira sighed and looked up at him. She stared into his eyes for a moment, before telling him what she was thinking, "Look, I'm a virgin. I want the first man I have sex with to be my husband." After she told him the hard facts, she watched for his reaction.

"That's fine. So, I guess this is to be continued until our wedding night then, huh?" he smirked, caressing the side of his face with the back of his hand. A smile crept upon her face, and her eyes lit up, growing wide.

"You mean you accept me even after I told you that?" she inquired, rubbing the side of his face.

"Yes. You aren't like other girls, you're special. I don't mind waiting on you. You're worth it." he kissed her on the forehead, causing her to smile just a tad bit harder.

Suddenly, Shatira grabbed him by the face and kissed him all over it. She then kissed him long and hard. She held him at arm's length, looking at him like he was the most amazing man in the entire world.

"Oh, I love you, baby, I love you so fucking much."

"I love you too, lil' momma," he brushed her hair out of her face, and stared at her face, marveling her beauty.

"So, what are we now? Are we still just friends or…"

"Fuck, nah," he shook his head, looking at her like she was crazy, "You my lady and future wife."

"So, you my man now, bae?" she looked at him with hopeful eyes.

"Fucking right. Hold on a sec'," he turned around and opened the drawer to the nightstand beside the bed. Reaching inside, he pulled out his gold chain which was attached to his name-plate, Menace. Turning back around to Shatira, he looped the chain over her head. Once he saw that the name plate on it was hanging crooked, he adjusted the chain on her neck so that it would be hanging correctly. "There you go, so mothafuckaz in the streets know it's official."

Shatira looked down at the chain in awe. She had the biggest smile on her face. She hadn't had a serious boyfriend before, and at that moment, she felt special. Little momma believed everything the young gangsta had told her. She could tell by the look in his eyes that he was keeping it one-thousand with her. And she'd planned on doing the same with him.

"Is this mine to have?" she asked of the chain as she looked at him, still holding on to that big smile of hers.

"Yeah, that's all you." he leaned in and kissed her tenderly on the lips. "Look up at me, sweetheart," as soon as he gave the command, she obliged him. "Now, that you're my lady, I'ma love you, honor you, cherish you, and make sure you don't want for nothing. You hear me?" she nodded, yes. "And if anybody puts their hands on you, that's they ass! I don't play about mine. I'm willing to kill and die over mine. And you're mine, right?"

Shatira looked at him with tears in her eyes, nodding yes to his question. She hadn't felt so much love from a man since her father. And since he was dead now, Menace was giving her what her heart desired.

"All I want from you is love, loyalty, truth and respect. You gemmie those things, and I'll give you the world...and everything in it. That's my word." he promised, holding her gaze, and meaning every word that rolled off his tongue.

"I got chu, little daddy."

"I got chu too, lil' momma."

Shatira and Menace kissed romantically. They then lay down in bed wrapped in one another's arms and staring up at the ceiling. They had love in their eyes and smiles on their faces. Menace kissed Shatira on her forehead, and then shut his eyelids. She followed shortly after. Five minutes later, they drifted off to sleep, dreaming about the life they'd share in years to come.

Chapter Eight

The next day

Menace pulled up inside of an alley just outside of a sports bar and placed the kickstand down, leaning the motorcycle aside. He dismounted the bike and pulled a black garbage bag from out of his back pocket. Looking up and down the alley to make sure there wasn't anyone watching him, he grabbed the ledge of the trash bin and hopped inside. Shatira watched as Menace flapped the garbage bag open and began stuffing it with empty beer bottles of a variety of colors: clear, brown, blue and green. Afterwards, Menace tied the bag into a knot and tossed it over to Shatira. He then hopped out of the trash bin and mounted the bike again. He kicked the kickstand up and used his leg to turn the motorcycle around as he walked it around into the other direction.

"What do we need all of these beer bottles for?" Shatira inquired, holding up the garbage bag and taking a look at it.

"I'm gonna teach you how to bust yo' gun, slim. If you gon' be my lady then you needa know how to handle yo' self. You Griff me?" Menace asked as he looked over his shoulder, both of his legs outstretched and touching the ground to balance the motorcycle. "You knowing how to defend yo' self is very important, 'cause one day, our lives may depend on it."

"I understand. If this is what I gotta do to be able to hold us down, then I'm with it. I want chu to always know I got cho back."

"And I got cho front, straight like that," he stuck his fist over his shoulder and she touched it with her fist. She then leaned forward and they kissed like a young couple, dangerously in love.

"That's what I'm talking 'bout, lil' momma," Menace fired his motorcycle back up and took off down the alley, making a left out of the end of it.

***

Menace and Shatira found themselves out in the woods. Shatira stood with her back to the motorcycle as she watched Menace. He held his gun in one hand as he reached inside of the garbage bag and pulled out the empty beer bottles he'd collected from out of trash bin inside of the alley. He lined the bottles up neatly on a log and retreated back to Shatira. He stepped behind her and placed the gun into her hands. Looking over her shoulder, he told her how to hold the firearm firmly with both hands.

"Alright, keep your finger outside of the trigger guard. You don't want your finger touching the trigga unless you ready to busta mothafucka'z brain!" Menace told her.

"I got cha," Shatira replied, with her head angled and one of her eyelids shut.

Menace then stepped out from behind her and showed her how to stand, with her legs apart. He also showed her the correct posture and how to aim.

"Yeaaah, there you go, just like that," Menace told her, smirking. "Now, breathe easy. I want chu to focus on the bottle you've set your sights on...concentrate. Imagine the bottle your focused on exploding as you pull the trigga."

Shatira did just like Menace had told her. It was like everything surrounding her no longer existed; even the noise of the outdoors had gone. Inside of her mind, the only two things that existed were herself and the green Heineken bottle she was focused on. She concentrated on the bottle really hard. Then, her finger slowly began to pull back on the trigger of the gun.

Blocka!

The Heineken bottle exploded in what looked like a million pieces and rained down on the ground. A smiling Menace looked from the broken pieces of glass on the ground to Shatira.

"That's what I'm talking about! Now, finish off the rest of the shits!" Menace commanded her.

Shatira had a determined and concentrated look on her face as she aimed the gun at the next bottle. After she took out the next bottle, she moved down the line of the bottles, pulling the trigger of her handgun.

Blocka! Shatter! Blocka! Shatter! Blocka! Shatter! Blocka! Shatter!

A broad smile stretched across Shatira and Menace's faces. They exchanged glances as she lowered the smoking handgun. Menace dapped her up and gave her mad props.

"I can't front, youa hell of a shot." Menace told her.

"Thanks, baby love." Shatira caressed the side of his face as she stared into his eyes, lovingly. She then leaned forward and kissed him. Pulling back, she kissed his lips again and brushed her nose across his nose, affectionately.

"Alright," he began, rubbing his hands together and looking at the garbage bag with the rest of the beer bottles in it. "Let's go another round, see if you're as good as we think you are." he started pulling beer bottles out of the garbage bag.

"Okay, then, line them up." Shatira tried to spin the handgun on her finger and accidentally pulled the trigger.

The gun fired and a bullet whizzed by Menace's ear, startling him. His eyes bulged and he grabbed his ear. He looked to his hand to see if he'd see blood, but there wasn't anything there. He then locked eyes with Shatira. She looked like was afraid for him until she realized she hadn't shot him. and she appeared to be afraid for him. She thought she's shot him. She then sighed with relief. The couple smiled at each other and then busted up laughing.

"Boyyyyy, I thought I shot chu!" Shatira doubled over laughing as she held her stomach.

"I did too. Thought my ass was gon' be disfigured and shit!" Menace leaned up against the tree, laughing.

"I almost had a heart attack," she brought her head back up and wiped away the teardrop that threatened to fall with her curled finger. She'd been laughing so hard that it brought tears to her eyes.

"Heart attack? Nigga, you nearly killed me! I oughta kick yo' lil' ass!" he charged over to her and they fought playfully. Having gotten out of breath, Menace wrapped his arms around Shatira and they fell on the ground. They rolled around on the around on the ground giggling and laughing, until he winded up on top of her. He stared down into her eyes. They held one another's gaze. Their laughing had ceased. He rubbed the side of her face with the back of his hand, then leaned down and kissed her.

That night

The Streets Don't Love Nobody

Fonzell stared out of the curtains watching Delores' house. He watched as her and her twin sons hopped into her Maybach and pulled out of the driveway. Once they were gone, he headed into the kitchen and unlocked the backdoor, letting Menace inside of the house. After he locked the door back, they walked into his bedroom. Fonzell stood by the door while Menace headed over to the closet, opening its door. The young gangsta pulled the drawstring and activated the light inside of the closet. He then pushed the clothes hanging on the rack aside and revealed a black digital safe. He unlocked the safe with his thumb print and pulled open its door, once it beeped.

There were shelves and shelves of stacks of money inside of the digital safe. This was all of the money Menace had saved during his tenure in the streets. He took care of the house, gave his pop his allowance and tricked on himself every now and again, but he saved majority of the dough he made out in the streets. He wasn't anyone's dummy, he knew with his lifestyle that a nigga always had to have some loot on deck, just in case he got caught up in some shit.

Fonzell's eyelids stretched wide open seeing all of those dead faces before his eyes. He couldn't help thinking that his son had as much money as a bank vault inside of his safe. Menace wasn't tripping off his old man seeing all the gwap he'd accumulated over the years because he knew he wasn't going to steal from him. All his pop had to do was ask and he was going to bless him with whatever amount of paper he wanted, just off the strength he was his old man.

"Pop, dump one of those pillows from outta their case on the bed and bring it to me. I need somewhere to put this money."

"Alright, junior," Fonzell did like his son told him. He stood on the side of him, holding the pillowcase open so he could toss whatever amount of money into it.

Menace started tossing in stacks of money into the pillowcase, back to back. Fonzell listened to his son count each ten thousand dollar stack in a hushed tone as he tossed them inside of the pillowcase.

"Alright, that should keepa nigga straight for a minute; you can close it now, pop." Menace told Fonzell once he dropped the last of the money into the pillowcase. He then turned around to shut the safe. Once he did, he took the pillowcase from his old man and tied it up. "Look here, pop, you need anything, you okay?"

"I could use a few dollars to get right and get a couple of thangs for the house. I mean, if it's not too much trouble, son." Fonzell told him.

"What chu talking about, man? It ain't never no trouble, I always got chu faded," Menace switched hands with the pillowcase and pulled out a small wad of blue face one-hundred dollar bills. He started off counting a few of them off, but then he just passed the entire wad to his father.

"All this for me?" he asked him with a raised eyebrow as he held the bills in his hand.

"Yeah, that's all you, OG."

"Thank you, son, I love you," Fonzell, still holding the wad of money, hugged his son and kissed him on the cheek.

"I love you, too."

The Streets Don't Love Nobody

"Listen, I don't mean to get all in your business or nothing, but what chu need all of that loot for?"

"Me and Shatira are out in these streets, pop. You know them hotels be expensive, so I need some cheese on deck." Menace explained to his father.

"Bring your ass back home, then. No sense in spending all that money on them hotels when you gotta perfect good house to lay your head at."

"I can't come back here until our *neighbors* are gone," he nodded his head to the right, which was where Delores' house was located.

"Shiiiit, we can take care of that now. Lemmie go get my strap," Fonzell went to go get his banga, but Menace grabbed him by his arm, stopping him.

"Nah, chill, pop. They gon' get their's, don't even trip," Menace assured him.

"Well, what chu have in mind?"

"I'll let chu know when the time comes."

"Alright."

"Come lemmie out the back door," Menace hoisted the pillowcase over his shoulder and headed towards the back door, with his father following closely behind.

***

Menace hit Big Meat up earlier that night to let him know he wouldn't be able to roll out with Flocka and Darnell to make the pickups. When the big man inquired about his not being able to roll out with the goons, he just told the nigga he

111

had something very 'important' that he had to handled that night. With the phone call having been made, Menace hit the streets to conduct some other business he had in mind.

Menace posted up outside of a 24 hour liquor store that had bright, colorful lights like a Las Vegas casino. He found himself occasionally glancing at the time on his cellular and looking up and down the street. As of right now, he was waiting for a nigga he'd been dealing with for quite some time. The fool he was supposed to be meeting up with was a jeweler, a ghetto jeweler. In fact, the jeweler he was about to connect with was the same one that had sold him and Flocka their jewelry. All of the ghetto jeweler's shit was legit and flawless, too. Homie had the hook up like Black & Blue, from the *I Got The Hookup* movie. He had the same merchandise they sold at the big time shops, but his shit was way cheaper.

Menace was about to pull his cellular out again to hit up his jeweler, but then he heard someone honking an awkward sounding horn. He looked down the block which was where he'd heard the horn coming from, and found a man wearing a helmet and riding a moped. Menace took his hand out of his pocket and approached the curb. Homeboy riding on the moped was his jeweler. He stopped the moped at the curb and turned off the engine. Dude then, removed his helmet and hung it on the handle bar of his moped.

"What's up, Menace?" The ghetto jeweler greeted Menace with a fist bump as he came around the moped.

"Damn, my nigga, it took you long enough. Shit." Menace complained. He was five minutes away from walking away, but then homie showed up.

"I'm sorry about that, G. I hadda drop my baby momma off some pampers and shit for my lil' one."

"Randy, nigga, yo' old ass gotta baby?" his forehead crinkled.

Randy, the ghetto jeweler, chuckled and smiled, showcasing the gold crowns on two of his teeth.

"I'm forty-seven years old, black man," Randy told him. He was a six-foot-three cat with a husky build. He rocked medium length salt and pepper dread locks, which he had pulled back in a band. He had on an overcoat which he wore over a button-down and slacks. The only piece of jewelry he had on was his high school class ring.

"Forty-seven?" Menace frowned up. He couldn't believe Randy was fifty-eight-years-old. He actually thought he was much younger, so he was surprised to hear he was older.

"Yep. Forty-seven." He smiled as he nodded.

"Wait, how old is yo' B.M?"

"My baby momma is twenty-six, bruh."

"Playa, playa," Menace smiled and dapped him up.

"Come on 'round here, man, lemmie show you what I got for you." Randy motioned for Menace to follow him, as he stepped off of the curb and unstrapped a jewelry case. Menace was standing beside him as he lifted the lid of the case, displaying hundreds of engagement rings. The rings were either platinum, white gold or gold. They all had flawless stones in them, and they twinkled.

"Nigga, you riding around with all of the merch' strapped to the back of yo' bike?" Menace asked like he couldn't believe he'd do such a thing. There were several lines going across his forehead.

"Heck yeah."

"You ain't worried about none of these knuckleheads out here tryna stick you for it?"

"Shit naw! I wish a mothafucka would try some shit," Randy looked to see if anyone was watching him. There wasn't anyone paying attention to him. He then held open his overcoat and showed off the .44 Magnum revolver tucked on his waistline. "And check this out, baby boy," he placed his dress shoe on the curb and lifted up his pants leg, showcasing the .38 secured in his ankle holster. Having showed Menace that he was packing, he let his pants leg fall back down over his holstered pistol and stood upright.

"My boy, you on yo' shit," Menace dapped Randy up again.

"Now, you see anything you like here?" Randy asked as he held open the case. His eyes scanned over the rings nestled in the velvet cushioning of the case. He was proud of the rings in his possession. Homie enjoyed being a salesman. Selling jewelry was his bread and butter. This was how he took care of his family.

Menace looked over the engagement rings, carefully. A smile spread across his lips when his eyes landed on the ring he'd planned to propose with.

"That one right there, with the canary yellow stone in the center," Menace nodded to the ring he had his eyes on.

Randy plucked the ring he believed Menace wanted out of the velvet cushion. He then showed it to him and said, "This it?"

"Yeah, that's her. She's perfect," Menace smiled reassuringly. "How much you want for her, though?"

"For you?" Randy stared down at the ring as he massaged his chin. He thought about how much he should charge Menace for the ring he wanted. Once he came to the conclusion, he looked back up at the young nigga. "Fuck it. Gemmie five stacks."

"My man," Menace smiled knowing he was getting a deal on the engagement ring. He reached inside of his pocket and pulled out a fat knot of dead presidents. He removed the rubber band and counted out the bread he was being hit with for the ring. While he was counting up the loot, Randy had his hand tucked inside of his coat. The ghetto jeweler clutched his gun and watched his surroundings with a keen eye. He was keeping a close eye on things in case niggaz were lurking in the shadows to rob them blind.

"Here you go," Menace hit Randy with the five racks. He then put the rubber band around the rest of the money in his possession and stuffed it back inside of his pocket. He watched as Randy lick his thumb and counted the money a second time. Once Randy had finished counting the money, he folded it up and stashed it inside of his pocket. "We good, my nigga?"

"Most definitely," Randy dapped up Menace. He then shut his jewelry case and strapped it back down on the back of his moped. Next, he strapped his helmet back on his head and mounted his moped. He cranked his motorized vehicle up and sped off. Homie got about fifteen feet down the street before throwing up two fingers, over his shoulder.

Menace grinned and cast his eyes down at the engagement ring he'd purchased. He then stuck the ring inside of his pocket and made his way toward his car. On his way back to the hotel room, Menace stopped to pick up some scented candles and half a dozen of red roses. Having procured these items, he headed back toward the hotel where Shatira was waiting for him.

      ***

Menace came through his hotel room's door with the bag of goods he'd purchased. He nudged the door shut with his elbow and wandered inside of the living room of the suite. He called out to Shatira and looked around for her. Once he heard her voice coming from the bathroom inside of their bedroom, he sat the bags down on the bed and approached it. Once he placed his ear to the door, he listened closely before addressing her again.

"Baby, you in there shitting, huh? Ol' shitty booty ass!" Menace chuckled, with the side of his face against the door.

"Hahahahahaha," Shatira laughed hardily. "No, bae, I'm in the shower. Why? You gotta twinkle?"

"Twinkle?" He asked, with his forehead crinkling. "Niggaz with small dicks twinkle. I'mma grown-ass man. I piss."

She chuckled and said, "Ok, well, do you have to piss, then?"

"Nah, I'm good, just being nosy."

The Streets Don't Love Nobody

"You wanna join me in the shower?"

"I'll take a rain check, baby. I got chu faded next time, okay?"

"Okay."

"I love you."

"I love you, too."

After having his conversation with Shatira, Menace grabbed the bags from off the bed and headed out into the living room. Once he turned out the light inside of the living room, he removed everything from the bags and went to work on his knees, with the surprise he had in mind. Once he was done, he pulled out his Bic lighter and struck a bluish yellow flame, lighting the stems of the candles, one by one. Once he was finished, he stuck the lighter into the small pocket above the pocket of his Dickies. Afterwards, he took the engagement ring out of his pocket and took a step back, admiring the scenery he'd created. A smile stretched across his face. He believed whole heartedly that Shatira was going to love his proposal.

"Alright, here goes nothing," Menace kissed the engagement ring.

When Menace heard the bathroom door inside of the bedroom open, he knew Shatira was finally out of the shower. Quickly, he straightened out the wrinkles in his clothing and brushed the imaginary lint from off his shoulders and arms. He then stood upright and cleared his throat with his fist to his mouth.

"Babe!" Menace called after Shatira.

"Yesssss, baby?" Shatira called back out, happily.

"Come here for a second, gorgeous."

"Okay. Just lemmie throw on something."

"Nah, come as you are."

"It'll just take me a second to put something on."

"Bring yo' ass, woman," Menace said playfully, wearing a smile across his lips.

"Alright, alright, alright."

A moment later, Menace heard Shatira's soft footfalls as she walked towards the living room. He looked to the bedroom door, just in time to see his lady's face when she saw what he'd laid out on the living room floor. Shatira eyes instantly filled with tears. She made an ugly face as teardrops dripped from the brims of her eyelids. She sniffled and fanned her eyes trying her best to dry the tears sliding down her cheeks. On the living room floor, spelled out in red rose petals was, *Will you marry me?* Placed around the words were burning candles.

Right then, Menace pulled out his cellular and programmed it to play Life Jennings' *Must be nice.* He set the cell phone down on the arm of the couch and took Shatira by the hand. He walked her over to the words he'd spelled out in rose petals at the center of the living room floor. Turning to her, Menace got down on one knee and held up the engagement ring.

"Shatira, you're all I want and need in this life. Will you do me the honor of being my wife?" Menace popped the question, hoping that she'd say yes.

The Streets Don't Love Nobody

More tears burst from Shatira's eyes as she stared down at the man she was madly in love with. She couldn't see herself growing old not being his wife, so she graciously accepted his proposal.

"Oh, yes, baby, yes. I'd married you a thousand times in just as many lifetimes. I love you so much," Shatira smiled as tears continued to pour down her cheeks in buckets. She watched as Menace slid the engagement ring onto her finger and then she stared at it, amazed at how beautiful it was. Looking up and finding Meance standing to his feet, Shatira jumped into his arms. She wrapped her arms and legs around him. They stared into one another's eyes, kissing tenderly for a minute. Then, they kissed long, hard and passionately.

Awww, to be young and in love.

Chapter Nine

Flocka coasted down the block looking left and right for Darnell. He finally found him parked at the center of the residential street. His arm was hanging out of the window and he was nodding his head to *Future*. Driving ahead, Flocka parked on the opposite side of the street from him, grabbed his gun and hopped out of the car. Slamming the door shut behind him, he adjusted his banga on his waist and made his way toward his charge. Advancing in his direction, Flocka saw Darnell adjusting his side view mirror to get a better look behind him. From the movement of his right arm he knew that he was grabbing his gun just in case whoever was approaching posed a threat.

"What's up?" Flocka cracked a smile.

"Flocka?" Darnell's forehead crinkled.

"Yeah, it's me, my nigga."

Darnell went silent and watched as he approached. Once he could clearly see that it was Flocka, he relaxed and took a breath.

"'Bouta say, my nigga, I was finna let this nine of mine get busy. I didn't know who you were moving through the shadows and shit."

"My fault," Flocka slammed the door shut after he'd gotten into the passenger seat. He then turned to Darnell and dapped him up.

"Don't wet it, my nig. It's all good," Darnell cranked up the old Honda Civic and looked to the side view mirror before he pulled out of the parking space.

The Streets Don't Love Nobody

"You mind if I put something in the air?" he plucked the half smoked blunt from behind his ear and held it up before Darnell's eyes. He'd been getting high on his way over and was dying to finish the session he'd gotten started.

"Long as you let me hit it, it's a go."

"Oh, fa sho'," he stuck the bleezy in his mouth and fished the Bic lighter from out of his pocket. Cupping his hand around the blunt, he struck a flame and took the time to light it. Afterwards, he tilted his head back and blew smoke into the air, polluting the interior of the vehicle. "So, what knucklehead was givin' you a headache when you picked up from whatever spot?" he passed him the blunt.

Darnell indulged in the weed and then blew out a cloud of smoke, responding, he said, "Mannnnn, I'ma take you to that spot last. That's the last spot we gon' make our pickup from. It's this nigga in there where they count up alla loot at. His name is Beast. He's in charge of making sure every coin that comes through there is accounted for. Anyway, I come up in there to get the bag, and I see this mothafucka stashin' a chunk of the take."

"Fuck outta here." Flocka said disbelievingly.

"Man, hell yeah. I tackled his big ass and we got to throwing hands. We tore that mothafucking count room up."

"You got in that ass, huh?"

"I'ma keep it all the way fonky witchu, 'cause that's what real niggaz do. I didn't put hands on that big swole mothafucka, but I managed to hold my own."

"Respect."

121

"Anyway, security ran up in there and broke us up. I got the bag and they sent homie home for the night."

"For the night? You mean to tell me that the nigga still working there?" Flocka asked with furrowed brows.

"Yep. And don't ask me how, either. 'Cause I thought fa sho' that nigga Richie was gone give that ass the boot, but his thieving ass is still up in there."

"Blood probably got some dirt on 'em."

"Gots to. There isn't any other way to explain the shit."

***

Darnell pulled up at the house which doubled as a ghetto gambling spot. He parked two houses down from it and murdered the engine. He and Flocka pulled out their guns from where they had them hidden inside of the vehicle. Out of habit they checked the magazines of them and smacked them back in.

"Follow my lead once we get in there. I doubt if this mothafucka tries something stupid again, but just in case, know what I'm saying?" Darnell said to Flocka.

"Fa sho'," Flocka nodded in response.

"Cool."

The two men hopped out of the car and made their way down the sidewalk, taking in the neighborhood. Everything was still and quiet, besides the sound of the crickets in the grass.

The Streets Don't Love Nobody

While Flocka was busy taking in their surroundings, turning his head from left to right, Darnell was walking ahead en route to the low key gambling spot.

"Come on. This the spot, right here." Darnell pushed open the gate. He left it opened as he crossed the threshold into the yard with Flocka bringing up his rear. Flocka followed him to the backyard, where he knocked on the backdoor. He and Flocka exchanged glances as they waited for someone to answer the door.

"Who is it?" a voice asked from the other side.

"Meat's people," Darnell answered.

A moment later, the door was unlocked and pulled open. The two men found themselves standing before a midget. He was a little fella with a head larger than his body. He was dressed in a snazzy blue suit and had a Thompson slung over his shoulder. This was Big Boi. He played the bouncer around the place. You know, making sure there was order in the establishment, and no one was giving the employees a hard time? Now, some may think Big Boi wasn't someone to be concerned with, but it would be wise to not let his appearance fool you. The little man had a reputation for busting ass and making niggaz come up off their tabs. The illegal gambling spot ran smoothly for the most part, and it was all thanks to that nigga, Big Boi.

"Flocka, what's up wit' it?" Big Boi asked as he touched fists with Flocka.

"Ain't shit. You know what time it is, I just dropped by to get that." Darnell told him.

"Yo', you know that shit that happened with Beast woulda never occurred if I was here. A nigga just so happened to be sick as a dog with the flu that night. Otherwise, homeboy wouldn't have gotten away without me bustin' a cap in his ass." Big Boi took his Thompson into both hands and pretended to bust on an imaginary Beast. He then lowered his weapon at his side. "You feelin' me?" he held out his fist.

"Sho' you right," Ronell dapped him up. "That mothafucka here tonight?"

"Yeah, he's here, and he's still handling the money, too." he reported regretfully.

"Get outta here! It's bad enough the nigga still working here, but he still onna money? Fuck is Richie's problem?"

"Man, you know that nigga Beast is his wife's nephew."

"Fa real?" Flocka's forehead creased.

"Hell yeah, homie, that nigga'z spot is cemented in here. As long as wifey suckin' and fuckin' boss-man real good, Beast is here to stay."

"Richie is a weak ass nigga, bruh." Darnell shook his head, thinking of how much of a pussy Richie, the owner of the illegal gambling spot was. "Where the fuck is he at anyway?"

"On vacay with his wife."

"Is that right? Well, who's runnin' the show then?"

"I'm keeping an eye on things, but a nigga can only do so much from up here. I have one of the fellas come up here while I go down there every now and again to check on things."

The Streets Don't Love Nobody

"Fuck is West? Isn't he the floor manager?"

"Yeah, but his ass got pinched a couple of hours ago with a burner."

"I swear to God, Richie's ass must have seven years of bad luck or something."

"Ain't that the truth."

Big Boi looked at Flocka like he just saw him standing there and then he turned his eyes back to Darnell, pointing his finger at Flocka, he said, "Who's ya man?"

"Oh, yeah, my fault, where's my manners? This my man, Flocka. Flocka this is Big Boi," He motioned to the little man holding the Thompson at his side.

Flocka threw his head back like *What's up?* And Big Boi returned the gesture.

Flocka glanced at his watch and looked to Darnell, saying, "You think we should head on down there to see what's brackin'?"

"Yeah, we should gon' 'head and see what's up." Darnell looked to Big Boi and said, "Yo', Big, I don't mean to be rude, but I'ma have to cut this lil' convo' short. I needa see about getting this money."

"Oh, you ain't bein' rude, man, gon' and handle yo' bitness. We can always shoot the shit later."

"Sho' you right," Darnell dapped up Big Boi.

Big Boi shut and locked the door behind Darnell and Flocka. He then motioned for them to follow him, and they fell in step behind him. They went down the hallway, through the foyer and entered the kitchen. Big Boi stopped at a black iron door and rung its door bell. The bell chimed and a moment later they could hear locks being undone. Next, the wooden door was being opened, and right after, the black iron door was being pulled ajar. The three men found themselves standing before a muscular man dressed in all black with Bouncer emblazoned across the chest of his shirt. His face was twisted into a scowl and he wore a holster strapped over his shoulders. In the holster there was a Desert Eagle Cross Shot.

Darnell and Flocka exchanged glances before he addressed the bouncer.

"Why yo' ass always got chu face frowned up, nigga? Knowing damn well youz as soft as baby shit," Darnell looked the bouncer up and down, like he was ready to shoot the fair one with him.

"What? Fool, you don't want these hands," Maul smiled and threw phantom punches at Darnell. A jovial expressed crossed Darnell's face as he threw some phantom punches back at him. The men's playful exchange left them both breathing slightly hard. They then dapped up and hugged. "'Sup, foolie? You here to pick up that bag, huh?"

"Sho' you right." Darnell nodded.

"Who this?" Maul looked to Flocka, with curiosity written across his face.

"This my man, Flocka," Darnell told him. "He's gonna be coming along with me for now on to pick up the loot and shit."

"'Sup, homie? Maul," the muscular bouncer dapped up Flocka. He showed him love because he fucked with Darnell, and Darnell fucked with niggaz just as cool as he was.

126

The Streets Don't Love Nobody

"'Sup with it?" Flocka greeted him.

"Y'all gon' 'head down," Maul moved aside to allow Darnell and Flocka to go down the staircase.

When Darnell and Flocka finally made their way down inside of the basement they found themselves in the middle of a   casino that looked like it belonged on a Las Vegas strip. There were two slot machines at every wall, four Black Jack tables, and a crap table at the center of the floor. 50 cent's *Get Money* played from the small speakers at the four corners of the room. The laughter and chatter of patrons mingled with the loud noises of slot machines. The sounds coming from the slot machines mimicked those of the arcades of the 80s and 90s era. Two sexy young women walked around scantily clad in bikinis serving drinks from silver platters. The occasional patron with slip bills of all denominations into their bikini bottoms.

The basement casino was like another world to Flocka. He continued to take in his surroundings as Darnell led him across the room. The young gangstaz found himself at a burgundy door which was on the left hand side of a window that looked like it belonged at a fast food drive-thru. Sitting at the window, on a stool before a counter, was a middle aged woman. She was dressed in a bowtie and black vest and her hair was pulled back in a ponytail. She exchanged nods with Darnell. Right then, Flocka gathered that the two knew each other. He figured it was due to Darnell's frequent pickups.

"This it?" Flocka asked.

"Yeah, this it," Darnell told him. "I don't expect any bullshit, but still be on yo' shit. You never know. You feel me?"

"Sho' you right." Flocka looked over his shoulders and adjusted his gun on his waistline.

Darnell knocked on the door in a specific pattern. He dropped his arm at his side and waited for the door to be answered. The rectangular slot in the door slid open and a pair of menacing eyes appeared. The pupils of the eyes moved from left to right, taking in the appearances of Darnell and Flocka.

"What's up, Darnell? Who this witchu?" Beast asked as he looked through the slot in the door.

"This my man, Flocka. He's gonna be picking that paypa up with me from now on. Now, come on now, open the door up," Darnell told him, growing agitated by the second. He didn't like Beast and it bothered him that Richie let him work in the count room after the incident.

Beast's eyebrows lowered, menacingly. "Hold on, homie. Don't go barking orders at me. You don't run shit up in here! You betta get somewhere with that fonky ass attitude!"

"My nigga, I ain't gon' tell yo' big ass again to open this door!" Darnell mad dogged him.

"If I don't open it, just what the fuck are you gon' do? Huh? What the fuck you gon' do?" Beast's eyebrows lowered further and his nose scrunched up.

"I don't know what the homie gon' do, but I'ma blast this door off its hinges and put one in yo' head. Straight up, homeboy." Flocka's eyebrows arched and his nostrils flared up. He lifted his shirt and showed gun, which was tucked in the front of his jeans.

Just then, the slot slammed shut and the door was unlocked and pulled open.

Flocka and Darnell found a skinny kid of average height standing before them. He didn't look to be a day over seventeen. He wore his hair in a close fade and had little facial hair to speak of. His attire was a black T-shirt which he wore a thin bulletproof vest underneath, an apron, and jeans. The youngsta also had a holstered handgun on his hip.

"What happened to the gangsta that was just at the door?"Flocka asked as he crossed the threshold inside of the room, with Darnell following closely behind him.

"Oh, he's still here!"Beast said from across the room, taking Flocka and Darnell off guard.

As soon as the kid that opened the door shut it, Flocka and Darnell found, Beast, the cornrow rocking brute who had initially answered the door. Homeboy was dressed exactly like the kid that had opened the door for Darnell and Flocka. His eyebrows were slanted and his jaws were locked. His head was slightly angled as he pointed a long barrel shotgun at them. Flocka and Darnell didn't seem to flinch seeing their lives threatened. The big son of a bitch may as well have had a goddamn cap gun as far as they were concerned.

"Now that you got that gun in my face, I hope you plan on using it." Flocka told him, looking him square in his eyes. He was frowned up and dying to draw his gun, but he was sure old boy would blast him halfway across the room before he cleared it from his waistline.

Chick! Chick!

Beast racked the shotgun, moving it back and forth from Flocka to Darnell. "Oh, I most def' plan on using it."

"Chill with that shit, Beast, we came to get that bag and then we outty," Darnell told him.

Beast trained his shotgun on Darnell and mad dogged him. He started to blast his ass across the room, but pushed that thought to the back of his mind. Taking a deep breath, Beast lowered his shotgun at his side. He grilled Flocka as he walked past Darnell, heading toward the table that the money was being counted on. There was a small pile of money on the table top along with a few stacks of money that had rubber bands around them.

Darnell walked over to the table and looked over the money. His forehead creased with lines. "Yo', I know this ain't all of the mothafucking paypa that's done came through that door tonight 'cause it's a full house." His forehead creased further and he turned to Beast. "Tell me this ain't what I'm 'pose to lay on Big Meat."

"Nah, that's not it. We put it in the safe; I'll get it for you." The kid, Myron, spoke up as he headed in Flocka's direction. Walking forward, he dug inside of his pocket and pulled out some keys, rifling through them as he continued toward the safe. Once he found the key he was looking for, he unlocked the safe in the far corner and removed the duffle bag, passing it to Darnell. Darnell held the bag in his hand and tested its weight, while holding Myron's gaze. Through their eyes they communicated that Beast had shorted changed the bag again.

Beast scowled at Myron seeing that he'd snitched on him. Pissed off, he went to blast him, saying, "You lil' dirty mothafucka!"

Before Beast could draw a bead on Myron, Flocka kicked the shotgun out of his hands and sent it flying across the room. Swiftly, Flocka snatched his gun off his waistline and shot him in the back of his kneecap. The bullet ripped through his flesh, broke bone, and came out of the side of his leg. Beast hollered out in agony and dropped to his wounded knee, howling in pain. He winced as he held his bleeding knee, soiling the carpet burgundy.

"Dirty mothafucka?" Darnell raised an eyebrow and looked at Beast. At this time, Flocka was walking around him with his gun pointed at his head. "You got some nerve calling me a dirty mothafucka, nigga."

"I let 'em think he convinced me to pull the lick. He strapped the money around my waist with duct tape…" Myron lifted up his shirt and exposed the stacks of dead presidents Beast had strapped around his waist. Grunting, he pulled the duct tape from around his waist and held it up like it was a money belt. "He planned on going to that McDonald's over on Broadway so he could gemmie my cut."

"Foul ass nigga," Darnell shot Beast a deathly look.

Myron pulled the stacks of money loose from the duct tape and dropped them inside of the duffle bag as Darnell held it open.

Someone knoking at the door drew everyone's attention, except Flocka's. He kept his eyes and gun on Beast, hoping he'd move a muscle so he could split his wig.

"I got it," Myron told Darnell as he headed to the door. He pulled open the slot in it and spoke to the guys standing on the opposite side of the door.

"We heard gunfire, y'all okay in there?" the head of the security team asked.

"Yeah, we straight, Big Meat's people just caught Beast stealing." Myron reported to them.

"For real? Again?"

"Real spit."

"Y'all need us?"

Myron looked back at Darnell who looked at Flocka. Without taking his eyes and gun off of Beast, Flocka responded, "Nah, we got this, tell 'em fall back."

Myron turned back around to address homeboy on the opposite side of the door. "Nah, we can handle it."

"Okay. Be sure to let boss-man know what's up."

"Fa sho'," Myron shut the slot in the door and walked back over to the safe. He shut the door of the safe and tugged on it twice to make sure it was closed. He looked back and forth between Darnell and Flocka, still pointing his gun at Beast's dome piece. "What're y'all gon' do with him?" he asked Darnell of Beast.

Darnell stared at a pitiful looking Beast; he didn't seem so hard then, bleeding all over the fucking place. Darnell then looked to Flocka, "Nothing comes to mind. What chu say, potna? You got any ideas what to do with Sticky Fingers?"

"Yeah. I know exactly what to do with this piece of shit," Flocka said, keeping his eyes glued on Beast. "Y'all grab his ass and bring 'em over to the table."

With the command having been given, Myron and Darnell dragged Beast over to the table. The stood behind him with their guns out, threatening to pop him if he tried something.

Flocka tucked his gun into the small of his back and looked around the room for a weapon. He smiled evilly once his eyes landed on the fire ax hanging on the wall. He hurried over to the axe and picked it up from its hooks. He gripped it with both hands and practiced swinging it. The ax whistled through the air as he swung it over and over again. Lowering the ax to his side, Flocka casually strolled over to table where Beast was. He smacked the small pile of money and loose bills from off the table top. Bills of all denominations went up into the air and floated down to the carpet, slowly.

"What the fuck? What chu finna do with that?" Beast's eyes became as big as saucers seeing the ax in Flocka's hand.

"This nigga left-handed or a right-handed, my nigga?" Flocka asked Myron. This was the same question Big Meat posed to Coolie, before he had him murdered for stealing from him.

"Lefty," Myron answered.

"Okay. Put that nigga hand down flat on the table."

"What? Awww, hell…" Beast was cut short when Darnell smacked him in the back of his head with his gun, dazing him. Darnell then tucked his gun on his waistline and held Beast as Myron placed his hand flat down on the table top. The big man was too dizzy to put up a fight.

"You know what they do to niggaz in third world countries that steal? Do you?" Flocka questioned, tapping the handle of the ax into the palm of his hand. He didn't wait for Beast's dizzy ass to give him an answer, he went on talking to him. "They chop off whatever hand they lifted someone else's goods with."

Flocka gripped the ax with both hands and hoisted it above his head. With a grunt, he brought the ax down with all of his might.

Thock!

The blade of the ax went through Beast's wrist bone and embedded its self into the table. Blood poured out of the thieving ass nigga'z stump as his hollered out in agony. That pink thing at the back of his throat shook and every tooth in his mouth was visible as he wailed loud enough to bursts everyone in the room eardrums. Right then, Flocka cocked his ax over his shoulder and swung it. It cut through the air and sliced Beast's neck open, spilling blackish blood on his shirt. His eyes were as big as tennis balls and his mouth quivered. Myron and Darnell stepped back and let Beast fall on the floor. They looked down at him. Myron crossed himself in the sign of the holy crucifix while Darnell looked at him like he was a stupid mothafucka for stealing again. "Y'all move back, Blood!" Flocka called out to them. As soon as they stepped back, he stepped forward and slammed the ax down into Beast's heart. He then stood over him and admired his handiwork. "Yo', call them niggaz that were at the door earlier and have 'em clean this bitch ass nigga up." He told Myron and then looked Darnell. "Come on, dawg, let's bail."

Flocka wiped off the handle of the ax with the lower half of his shirt and headed for the door. He and Darnell left out and walked across the casino floor as if they didn't leave in a nigga dead in the count room.

***

The Streets Don't Love Nobody

"Dawg, you did that nigga Beast something awful," Darnell said as he and Flocka came out of the yard of the low key gambling spot. He was en route to his car with Flocka walking beside him.

"I had to do what I hadda do to let that nigga know Big Meat ain't accepting no shorts out here." Flocka told him.

"Fa sho," he popped the trunk and Flocka dropped the duffle bag inside of it. He then slammed it shut and smacked imaginary dirt from off his hands.

"Yo,' you tryna get something to eat? I'm hungry as a hostage."

"Yeah, I could eat. What chu got in mind?" Darnell slammed the door shut and stuck his key inside of the ignition.

"I don't know, man. A nigga starving, whatever's close," Flocka slammed the passenger door shut.

"Shiiiiiit, the only spot I know around here is Mickey D's, my nigga."

"Well, Mickey D's it…"

Blatatatatatatatat!

A wave of automatic gunfire ripped through the air and punctured what looked like one hundred holes through the driver's door and windshield. The windshield had several cobwebs in it from the glass breaking due to the rapid gunfire. There was blood splattered all over the inside of the broken windshield as well as the door panels and interior.

Darnell and Flocka lay still inside. The smell of blood and gun smoke lingered in the air, making the presence of Death obvious and overwhelming.

A moment later, the gunman came running over, switching hands with the AR-15 he'd used to lay down the murders. Using his leather gloved hand; he reached inside of the vehicle and popped the trunk. Running to the rear of the car, he snatched out the duffle bags that Darnell and Flocka had collected along Big Meat's routes. Afterwards, he ran over to the passenger side to see if he'd left anyone alive to tell the tragedy that had occurred that night. Looking inside, he saw Flocka's eyelids flicker open. That's when the gunman pulled out the gun on his waistline and pointed it. Flocka squeezed his eyelids shut and threw up his arms to shield his face.

Blocka!

Chapter Ten

A couple of nights later

He lay in bed still. Eyelids shut, mouth closed, chest rising and falling as he breathed. He was in a hospital gown underneath sheets. The lights were out. In fact, the only light that could be seen was the one shining inside of the room from the hallway. Although the light wasn't much, it was enough to outline the upper half of his body. The medical machinery beside his bed made their respective noises as they kept track of his vitals and monitored his heart. He had several cuts that covered his face and the side of his neck. At that moment, a fly flew around the room aimlessly, making that annoying sound that flies make. It eventually landed on his cheek and inched its way up, rubbing its hands together.

Just then, the doorway was filled with three dark figures. They made their way inside of his room. The largest of the three picked a news paper up from off the push-table and rolled it up snuggly. The dark figure's shadow eclipsed the man lying in bed, watching the fly as it crept its way up onto the bed ridden man's right eyelid. The dark figure stood where he was clutching the news paper and watching the insect.

Wap!

The news paper smacked against the bed ridden man's face and the fly flew away. This caused the man wearing the gown, which was Flocka, to frown up and flutter his eyelids. As he peeled his eyelids open, he was met by several more smacks against his face. The assault from the news paper came back to back, rapidly. Before the assailant knew it, Flocka was swinging his arms and kicking his legs. The dark figure threw the news paper at his head and it deflected off his forehead, falling to the linoleum.

Flocka stopped flailing his arms and legs. Through narrowed eyelids, he tried to make out the two men at the head of his bed. At that moment, the light switch was flipped *on* and Flocka narrowed his eyelids even further. He tried his best to make out the men being that his vision hadn't come into focus. Once his sight did return to normal, he found himself staring at Bumpy and two of Big Meat's goons.

"Grab this nigga'z arms!" Bumpy looked to the goons standing to either side of him. On his word, they moved to grab either of Flocka's arms. He tried swinging on them, but none of his punches connected. One of them cracked him in the jaw and left him in a daze. He was left swinging blindly, then. Seeing their chance, the goons grabbed his arms and restrained him.

"Lemmie go, Blood! Y'all niggaz get y'all fucking hands off me!" Flocka struggled to break free of the goons hold, but his efforts were in vain.

"Nigga, calm yo' bitch ass down, 'less you want me to carve yo' eyes outta yo' fuckin' head up in here!" Bumpy said through clenched jaws as he pulled out a knife he'd fashioned out of plastic. He knew he and the goons wouldn't be able to sneak their guns in through the metal detectors, so he came up with the idea of crafting knifes out of plastic and sneaking them inside of the hospital. Now, they weren't as good as a few handguns, but they were definitely better than nothing.

"Yo', man, fuck is this all about?" A scowling Flocka demanded to know.

The Streets Don't Love Nobody

"The money. Where the fuck is the gwap at, huh?" Bumpy asked him, rubbing his finger and thumb together in reference to money. He was talking about the duffle bags of dead presidents that Darnell and Flocka had collected along Big Meat's routes.

"I don't know. And how should I? The last thing I remember was that nigga Darnell's ride gettin' Swiss Cheesed, and here I am now."

"Bullshit!"

"Nigga, ask Darnell, then."

"That's gonna be pretty fuckin' hard bein' that he's dead."

"Dead?" Flocka's forehead creased. He hadn't known that Darnell had been murdered. It kind of saddened him because he seemed like a pretty cool dude. He'd planned on fucking with him outside of business, but unfortunately that wouldn't be happening now given the circumstances.

"Yes, nigga, dead," Bumpy told him again, spelling it out. "D.E.A.D. Dead. He's gone, and so is all of the money y'all collected on Big Meat's routes."

"Wait a minute. I know Meat ain't thinkin' that I had somethin' to do with it. I mean, look at the condition I'm in, 'cause of this shit. I'm banged up and laid up in here and…" Flocka's words died in his throat. He'd just noticed that his left leg was missing. You see, when the gunman had sprayed Darnell's car, one of the jacketed bullets from his AR-15 had mutilated Flocka's leg. The doctor tried to save it in surgery but there wasn't anything they could do to reserve it. The limb was as dead as Darnell's ass was and it had to be amputated. "My-my leg-what the fuck happened to my leg?" he stared

139

down at his missing limb underneath the sheets. He couldn't believe it was gone. It was making sense to him now. The reason he'd wakened up so out of it with a fog over his brain was because he had been put to sleep in order to perform the amputation.

"Fuck yo' pussy ass leg, nigga! We want that paypa, and we not leavin' out this bitch 'til we get it. So, I suggest you gemmie its whereabouts before you find yo' self a double amputee out this mothafucka," Bumpy threatened as he pulled out a second plastic knife. When Flocka looked down and seen them, his heart quickened inside of his chest. In his position, plus being weakened, he knew he didn't have the strength to fight Bumpy and the goons off, so he knew he should try to at least reason with him.

Flocka shut his eyelids briefly and took a deep breath. He then went on to speak to Bumpy as coolly and calmly as he could, "I don't know where that money is at. All I remember is gettin' blasted on, and then I woke up in here. I take it that whomever the fool was that sprayed the car took the loot we'd collected for Big Meat."

For a minute Bumpy stood at the foot of the bed staring at Flocka. He didn't have to say a word; Flocka knew the little nigga was reading him. He was also weighing his options. He could leave Flocka right where he'd found him...dead, or he could let him live in hope that he'd come up with the stolen loot.

Having decided that he believed Flocka, Bumpy stuck one of the plastic knives in his waistline and pulled out his cellular, speed dialing Big Meat. As the cell phone began to ring, he placed it to his ear.

The Streets Don't Love Nobody

"Boss dawg, what's happenin'?" Bumpy spoke into his cellular. "Yeah, I got our lil' friend right here. He claims he doesn't know where our prize is. Now, call me crazy, but I believe 'em." Bumpy cradled his cell phone to his ear with his shoulder, listening to what Big Meat was saying as he cleaned the dirt from underneath his fingernails with the plastic knife. He said 'unh huh' a few times as he listened to what he was being told. He then held the hand of the nails he was cleaning before his eyes and examined them. Next, he blew out the particles of dirt he saw remaining around his nails and went back to cleaning them. "Alright, hold on."

Bumpy walked over to Flocka and placed his cell phone to his ear. He held it there as he talked to Big Meat.

"It's like I told Bumpy, nigga blasted on us and took the loot," Flocka told him. He then listened to everything that the crime boss had to tell him.

Big Meat took a deep breath before beginning, he said, "I hear what chu saying, youngsta, but fuck all that. My paypa got taken and its gon' have to be accounted for. I sent chu out with homeboy, and y'all got taken for them grips. Y'all responsible for mines as soon as its in yo' possession. Dude is dead, so that means the weight falls on yo' shoulders. So, check this out, hit them streets and find my money. Or them people gon' find yo' ass…floating face down in a river." With that having been said, Flocka nodded to Bumpy and he took the cellular away from his ear. He watched the little nigga chop it up on the cell phone as he stuck the plastic knife on his waistline.

"Alright. I got chu. Peace," Bumpy said to Big Meat before disconnecting the call. He then focus his attention on Flocka. "Okay, my nigga, you heard the man. Soon as yo' ass is released, you touchin' 'em streets, and you gon' find that bag or that's yo' skinny black po' ass. Take it easy," he patted Flocka on his last leg and looked to the goons. "We out this bitch." He motioned for them to follow him with a wave of his hand and made his way toward the door.

As soon as Bumpy and his goons left out of his room, Flocka sighed with relief and laid back in his bed. Staring up at the ceiling, he knew his ass was going to be in big trouble if he didn't get that money into Big Meat's possession…fast.

The next day

The orderly rolled Flocka out in his wheelchair and he met the beaming sun. He narrowed his eyelids and held his hand above his brows, looking around. He had a gut feeling that some of Big Meat's goons were going to jump out of nowhere and snatch his ass up, but that threat never materialized. Acknowledging that he was in the clear, Flocka told the orderly to lock the wheelchair in place so he could get up. Once the orderly obliged him, he got upon his feet and approached the curb.

As soon as Cee Cee pulled up in front of the entrance of the hospital, Flocka hopped into the front passenger seat and slammed the door shut behind him. He looked to Cee Cee to find her chewing bubble gum. Her brows furrowed and she tilted her shades down to make sure her eyes weren't deceiving her.

"Baby, what happened to yo' leg?" Cee Cee questioned with concern.

"Hold on a second, ma," Flocka turned from her and looked to the orderly that had rolled him out to the curb in the wheelchair. He threw up his hand by the way of saying goodbye. The orderly told him to take it easy as he turned the wheelchair around to head back inside of the hospital. As soon as the double electric doors shut behind the orderly, Flocka's face twisted in anger and he clenched his jaws, causing them to pulsate. He then turned back around to Cee Cee. "What happened to my leg? You happened to my leg, you stupid bitch!"

Blatatatatatatatat!

A wave of automatic gunfire ripped through the air and punctured what looked like one hundred holes through the driver's door and windshield. The windshield had several cobwebs in it from the glass breaking due to the rapid gunfire. There was blood splattered all over the inside of the broken windshield as well as the door panels and interior.

Darnell and Flocka lay still inside. The smell of blood and gun smoke lingered in the air, making the presence of Death obvious and overwhelming.

A moment later, the gunman came running over, switching hands with the AR-15 he'd used to lay down the murders. Using his leather gloved hand; he reached inside of the vehicle and popped the trunk. Running to the rear of the car, he snatched out the duffle bags that Darnell and Flocka had collected along Big Meat's routes. Afterwards, he ran over to the passenger side to see if he'd left anyone alive to tell the tragedy that had occurred that night. Looking inside, he saw Flocka's eyelids flicker open. That's when the gunman pulled out the gun on his waistline and pointed it. Flocka squeezed his eyelids shut and threw up his arms to shield his face.

Blocka!

Darnell's head launched backwards, slamming into the driver's window. His brain fragments and blood splattered against the window and the dashboard. A gaping hole was in the center of Darnell's forehead as he stared out at nothing. He was dead to the world.

Once Flocka realized he hadn't been shot, he peeled his eyelids opened and looked around. He discovered the gunman fleeing down the block. He watched as he jumped into the getaway car and peeled away from the scene of the murder. Flocka opened the passenger door and fell out onto the sidewalk. He heard the police sirens wailing in the distance, as he grimaced and tried to get upon his feet. He managed to get upon his right leg, but ended up falling right back down. Lying where he was, he looked down at his left leg and saw it was bloody and mangled.

"Fuck, my leg! My mothafucking leg!" Flocka cried out as he held his banged up limb, blood seeping between his fingers. "Aarrrrrr! Fuuuuuck!"

"I thought you said yo' pop was a sharp shoota in Nam and taught cho ass how to shoot!"

Flocka screamed on Cee Cee.

"He did!" Cee Cee swore, looking scared as shit. Flocka's eyes were ablaze and she was afraid he was going to kill her. At the moment, he didn't seem anything like the smooth talking thug she'd met that warm sunny day with her homegirl, Shatira.

"You lyin'! Shut the fuck up!" Spit flew from off Flocka's lips as he slammed his elbow into Cee Cee's face, breaking her shades and her nose at the same time. Blood spurted out of her nostrils upon impact. Before she could mount a defense, Flocka was grabbing her by the back of her neck and slamming her forehead into the steering wheel. When she threw her head back, her eyelids were fluttering and the lower half of her face was bloody. She broke down crying and held her hands to her face, smearing them in blood.

"I'ma mothafuckin' gimp 'cause of you! Fuck I'm 'pose to do now, Blood? Collect S.S.I or some shit? Huh?" Flocka looked over at her, and she was still crying and holding her face. He sighed and shook his head, popping open the glove-box. He snatched the few napkins out of it he saw and threw them at Cee Cee, saying, "Clean yo' fuckin' self up!"

Cee Cee winced as she began wiping the blood from off her face as best as she could. Once the napkins were soiled on one side, she folded them in half and started wiping with the clean side. She then placed flapped the sun visor down so she could take a look at herself through the rectangle shaped mirror. Seeing a few traces of blood on her face, she wiped it off and balled up the stained napkins. She smacked the sun visor closed and threw the balled up napkins out of the window.

"Alright, now start this motahfucka up and take me to my money!" Flocka commanded Cee Cee with an evil eye. He then watched as she put the Impala in drive and drove out of the hospital's parking lot.

Flocka felt underneath the seat and on the side of it, coming up empty handed. He frowned and looked to Cee Cee. "Yo', where my strap at?"

"I forgot to bring it."

"You forgot to bring it? With this shit I'm mixed up in, I needa be strapped 24/7. I can't be caught slippin'. Look, check this out, after we scoop up the loot, you slidin' me by the house so I can get that thang. You got that?"

"Yeah, I got it," Cee Cee assured him. She couldn't believe he had the nerve to order her around after beating her ass. As bad as she wanted to go upside his head, she was going to fallback. To go against him in his current mind state wouldn't be wise, because he was liable to beat her ass to death.

"Good. Now, push this bitch to our destination," Flocka demanded as he fished the roach end of blunt out of the ashtray and fired it up. He took a pull off of it and blew out a cloud of smoke. He then focused his attention out of the passenger window, watching the scenery change before his eyes as he indulged in some gas.

Unbeknownst to Flocka, an livid Cee Cee was watching him out of the corner of her eyes. Occasionally, she'd glance back at the windshield.

This nigga got me fucked up, if he thinks he's gonna put his hands on me and ain't shit gon' happen to 'em! I ain't no punk bitch! You gone regret the day you laid yo' mothafucking ball scratchers on me! Best believe that, bitch nigga! Ummmhmmm, watch and see! I got something for that ass, Cee Cee nodded slightly and focused her attention back on the windshield. A roguish smirk etched across her lips.

"Fuck is you smilin' about?" Flocka asked suspiciously.

"Nothing," Cee Cee shook her head. The smile had vanished from her face.

"Lemmie tell you somethin', sweetheart. I don't know what chu thinkin' up there," he tapped his finger against her temple. "but get it the fuck out cha head 'cause should you try me, I'm blow yo' lil'pretty ass away. You got that?"

"I understand."

"Good," Flocka took the blunt out of his mouth and blew a cloud of smoke in her face. She stared ahead acting as if he hadn't blatantly disrespected her.

A slight frown formed on Cee Cee's brow and she bit her inner jaw, gripping the steering wheel so tight her knuckles turned white. She was hot. I mean, real hot, but some couldn't get some get back until she was sure she had the upper hand. So, as for right now, she had to play good slave to master until she found her opening.

***

Cee Cee pulled one house down from a Spanish stucco house with a dirt patched lawn and slightly rusted fence. The outside of the house was sprawled with graffiti and its windows and doors were boarded up. Cee Cee killed the engine of the Chevrolet Impala and pointed to the house, letting Flocka know that the money was stashed there.

"Why you stash the shit here instead of keepin' it at cho place?" Flocka's forehead crinkled.

"For all I know yo' people could have suspected something suspicious, and came looking for my ass. Now, if they decided to come to my house, looking for some paypa and found it, I know they would of smoked my motha, my father, my lil' bro and me."

Flocka stared ahead at nothing as he nodded and massaged his chin. He agreed with what Cee Cee had done in regards of the money. Little momma was right. Had Big Meat

147

sent Bumpy and his goons to homegirl's house, then they would have taken the money and executed everybody in that mothafucka.

"Alright, take me up in here so I can get them dead faces," Flocka told Cee Cee as he opened the passenger door. She hopped out the whip with him. Together, they made their way to the Spanish stucco house. They made their way around the side of the house and into the backyard, where she took off the large wooden board that was covering the back door. She sat the board aside and opened the black screen door, entering. Flocka crossed the threshold inside of the house. He and Cee Cee made their way through the kitchen looking around it. Having made it inside of the living room, the first thing he noticed were the piles of flies at the corners of the windows' seals. Then there was the carpet. The carpet had been stripped from the floor to display the hardwood floor underneath it, which was dusty and scarred. The walls were dirty and had gang graffiti on them. There were empty beer cans, liquor bottles, plastic cups and burned out candles on the floor. Flocka reasoned that some niggaz and a couple of bitchez had busted inside of the place and had a party.

"Its in that door up there." Cee Cee pointed at a small door in the ceiling, as she stood beside Flocka.

"Now, how in the fuck are we 'pose to get up there to get it?"

"The same way I got it up there, a ladder. Wait here. It's in the other bedroom," she went to recover the ladder, but Flocka grabbed her by her arm, stopping her in her tracks. She looked back at him.

"Hold up. I'm goin' in there witchu, for all I know you gotta banga in there. Unh huh, a nigga stay up on it," he

148

tapped his finger against his temple as he followed her inside of a nearby bedroom.

Cee Cee retrieved an old raggedy ladder that didn't look too sturdy. She carried the ladder back inside of the living room and planted it in the center of the floor, opening it up. Afterwards, she climbed the ladder, each bar of it squeaking as she stepped upon it. Once she made it to the door in the ceiling, she pushed it upward and over. Next, she pulled out her cellular and used its flashlight, shining it over the floor. She smiled when she saw two of the duffle bags. Leaving the flashlight of her cell phone on, she sat it aside and grabbed one of the duffle bags.

"Alright, I'm gonna toss one down now, okay?" Cee Cee called down to Flocka.

"Alright," Flocka replied, looking up at her from where he was standing. A moment later, she was tossing the duffle bag down to him. He caught the bag and hurriedly unzipped it, peering inside of it. When he saw the stacks and stacks of dead white men in the bag, a smile broadened his face. He zipped the bag back up and tossed it aside. Next, he looked back up at Cee Cee. She was looking down at him and holding the last duffle bag downward for him to catch it. He held up his hands to catch the duffle bag.

"Alright, drop that mothafucka!" Flocka said with his awaiting hands held up to catch the duffle bag.

"Okay," Cee Cee called down to him, releasing the duffle bag. Flocka caught the falling bag. When he looked back up, he met Cee Cee's mad dog stare and a black handgun. His eyes got as big as saucers and he dove to the floor, just as the first shot was fired. The shot struck the hardwood floor and dust flew up into the air. Flocka landed on his side wincing, still holding the duffle bag. Looking back up, he saw Cee Cee turning her gun to fire at him again. Swiftly, he kicked the raggedy ladder that she was on, sending it falling and her hurling toward the floor. She crashed to the hardwood floor, frowning in pain. Her handgun, which she'd pulled out of the last duffle bag, slid across the floor spinning in circling. It stopped once it bumped up against the wall.

"Ol' thot ass bitch, tried to put one in a real nigga head, huh? Well, I got somethin' for yo' triflin' ass hoe!"

Flocka swore from the other side of the room. Getting up on her hands and knees, Cee Cee looked his way and found him speed walking in her direction. His fists were balled tight and he had madness dancing in his eyes. As soon as he reached her, he cocked his leg back and kicked her in the stomach, knocking the wind out of her. The impact from the blow lifted her off her hands and dropped her on her back. Flocka stood over her and stomped the dog shit out of her ass. His sneaker came down fast and hard, slamming into her chest and stomach. In a desperate attempt, Cee Cee snatched off his prosthetic leg and left him hobbling on his last leg. "Oooooh, shiiit!" Flocka's eyes grew big; flapping his arms like a bird would its wings and trying to keep his balance on one leg. He lost his equilibrium and fell hard to the hardwood floor, landing on his side.

Cee Cee tossed the prosthetic leg aside and crawled for the handgun as fast as she could. While she was moving toward the gun, Flocka was crawling towards his prosthetic leg. As Cee Cee was grabbing her gun and turning around to shoot Flocka, he was grabbing his plastic leg. She was pulling the trigger of her banga as the fake limb was hurled at her. The prosthetic struck the gun out of Cee Cee's hand and sent it sliding across the floor again. Flocka hopped upon his good leg and hopped after Cee Cee, plastic limb in his hand. He found her crawling toward the gun. By the time she picked it up and turned around, Flocka was already on top of her. With a grunt, he knocked the gun out of her hand with his fake leg. He then kneeled down to the floor and started cracking her upside the head with it. Seeing that Cee Cee was dizzy and barely conscious, Flocka picked up his gun and straddled her. He pressed the banga beneath her chin and turned his head so her blood wouldn't splatter against his face, squeezing his eyelids shut.

"Eat lead, bitch!" Flocka told Cee Cee as he went to blow her brains out.

"No, wait, wait, wait, wait!" Cee Cee pleaded, with her eyes bulging and her hands up. "Please, please, don't kill me! I'll do anything you want me to do! I'll suck yo' dick and let chu fuck me in every hole! I swear to God, just don't kill me, please!" she said with tears welling up in her eyes.

Flocka stared down into Cee Cee's face, still pressing the gun beneath her chin. From the look in his eyes she could tell he was thinking things over. "Ok, I'ma let chu up, and you betta suck this big black mothafucka like yo' life depended on it, which is fuckin' does."

Flocka held the gun to Cee Cee as he reached over and grabbed his prosthetic leg. He kept his eyes on her as put the plastic limb back on and adjusted it so it would stay on his stump. Next, he got to his feet and pulled Cee Cee upon her knees. Pointing his gun at her, he unzipped his jeans and pull out his meat. He stroke his dick until it was standing its longest and strongest, veins bulging all over it. Wearing an evil grin, he motioned Cee Cee over to him with his gun so she could suck him off. She came over to him on her knees and grabbed his dick, stroking it up and down. Shortly, semen oozed out of the bulbous head of his penis. She stuck out her tongue, and went to bring it to the head of his dick, when he pressed his gun into her temple. Instantly, she looked up into his eyes, frowning and wondering what he was about to do to her. Flocka eyebrows were arched and his nose was scrunched up. His teeth were clenched, and a vein pulsated at his temple.

"Watch cho mothafuckin' teeth while you at it. I swear 'fore God, Blood, if yo' fuckin' teeth graze my shit, I'ma leave yo' thoughts stuck to the ceilin'. You hear me?" Flocka asked, meaning every word of the threat.

Cee Cee nodded. Using her tongue, she swirled his cum around his dick-head, and then took it inside of her slopping warm mouth. Flocka and Cee Cee held one another's gaze as she sucked his dick properly. Her hot saliva rolled down his engorged dick and mingled with his hairy nut sack. Cee Cee eyes stayed locked on Flocka as she handled her business, looking at the pleasured expression on his face.

Flocka shut his eyelids and threw his head back, licking his lips and moaning in delight. "Yeah, that's it, bitch. Suck it! Suck the skin off this mothafucka," he placed his hand on the top of her head and began humping her mouth. A look of ecstasy was plastered across his face and he looked to be having himself a good old time, hearing her gag on the end of his pole. Cee Cee grabbed hold of his slightly hair asscheeks as he mouth fucked her. "Uh, uh, uh, yeah, that's it! That's it! Right there, I'm 'bouta pop! I'm 'bouta pop all in yo' mothafuckin' mouth, on the set!"

Flocka deliver one last thrust and held his dick deep down inside of Cee Cee's mouth, leaving his nut sack hanging down against her chin. Clenching his jaws, he looked down at her as he splashed his seeds inside of her grill. Cee Cee squeezed her eyelids shut as she felt the warm spunk filling her mouth. She gagged a little and tried to move, but Flocka held her in place.

"Don't move, don't chu fuckin' move! Uh, uh," Flocka grunted, humping her mouth three more times and emptying every drop of semen in his nut sack he had to offer. "Ahhhh, shit, that felt good as fuck, Blood! Damn." Keeping his eyes on Cee Cee, Flocka slowly pulled out his limp dick and it dropped between his legs. His flaccid meat glistened as it hung in place, dripping semen to the floor. Switching hands with his gun and pointing it back at Cee Cee, Flocka reached inside of his back pocket and pulled out his red bandana. He wiped off his meat and threw the bandana over his shoulder.

Afterwards, he ordered little momma to turn around and pull her pants and panties down. As she performed the task he'd given her, he stroked his dick back to its full potential. In no time, he'd rocked back up, and was ready to fuck something. "Bend over and grab yo' ankles!" Flocka ordered Cee Cee. She obliged. Still stroking his grown man, he observed her big old booty and her tight asshole. The sight of it made his dick slightly harder. He loved fucking bitches in their ass, it made him feel empowered.

"Ooooh, yeaaah, look at that asshole, that mothafucka is beautiful," Flocka smiled sinisterly as he looked down at Cee Cee's asshole. Getting down on his knees, he fucked her asshole with his tongue, pressing it further and further into her opening. Cee Cee winced a little, but she didn't dare fight him off for fear he'd blow her brains out like he'd promised. Flocka loosened up Cee Cee's opening as much as he could with his tongue. He then spat two globs of spit directly on her asshole. Afterwards, he stood straight up and stroked his dick, tapping it against her asshole. Licking his lips, he pressed the head of his dick against Cee Cee's asshole. The width of his penis stretched her hole wider and wider as it inched inside of her rectum. Tears came to her eyes and she bit down hard on her bottom lip, feeling her void being filled to capacity. As bad as she wanted him to stop, she was going to keep her mouth shut. The last thing she wanted to do was have that nigga flip out and puff her wig out. She'd rather suffer through the pain and get it over with.

"Aaaahh, yesss, yo' mothafuckin' asshole is hot! This mothafuckin' tight, too! On Bloods!" Flocka said, looking down at his dick as it slowly went in and out of Cee Cee's butthole. The more he thrust himself in and out of her, the more of her shit accumulated on his dick. The shit on his dick made it easier for him to slide in and out of her booty hole. He was moving slow at first, but now he was moving faster, and his pelvis was smacking against her buttocks. While he was smashing her out from the back, Flocka reached over and grabbed a handful of Cee Cee's hair, pulling her head back. He then pressed his banga to the back of her head. She winced as tears cascaded down her cheeks. Her bottom lip quivered, and she sniffled, trying her best to ignore the ring of fire surrounding the entrance of her rectum.

"Uh, uh, uh, uh, uh!" Flocka pummeled Cee Cee from behind, feeding her anus with his dick. "Oh, fuck, I'm 'bouta cum, I'm 'bouta mothafuckin' cum!" he gripped Cee Cee's meaty hips and threw himself into her three more times, grinding inside of her. As he ground against her, he busted all inside of her asshole. He then threw his head back, shutting his eyelids and smiling in satisfaction. Looking down, he slowly withdrew himself out of Cee Cee's anus. His dick hung limply, dripping shit, semen and bloody from it on the hardwood floor. "Damn, that shit there hit the spot."

The Streets Don't Love Nobody

Flocka switched hands with the gun again; he then snatched the bandana from off his shoulder and cleaned his dick off. Right after, he tossed his stained bandana to Cee Cee. As he pulled his pants back up on his waist and zipped them back up, he watched her clean herself up. Once she was done cleaning up the mess Flocka had left behind, she pulled up her panties and pants, zipping them up. She turned around to Flocka slowly, moving like she had a broomstick up her ass, but really she was in a hell of a lot of pain.

"Good lookin' out, that was fiyah," Flocka flashed her a smile and tucked his gun at the front of his pants. Looking up at her, he didn't see the pleased facial expression that he was wearing, but he didn't a fuck. He was fucking her up the ass for her pleasure. Nah, he was banging her up the ass for his own enjoyment. As far as he was concerned, fuck that bitch! She cost him his leg and had even tried to put a bullet in him. The way he saw it, she didn't have any love for him, so he for damn sure didn't have any love for her punk ass. "Alright, I'ma let chu live, but from now on, you do what I say when I say it. And if you fuck up this time, I'm comin' to yo' house and I'm killin' everything and everyone that chu love, you understand?" Cee Cee didn't say a word which angered him. Pissed off, Flocka pulled out his gun and pointed it at her forehead. Instantly, tears threatened to drip from her eyes and she raised her hands in the air. Her entire body shook nervously, wondering if he was going to pop her ass like a zit. "I said, do you fuckin' understand?" His nostrils flared and his chest inflated and deflated, angrily. He looked like he was about a minute away from murdering her ass on the spot.

"Yes, yes, I understand, just, please, please, don't kill me," Cee Cee begged for her life, with her trembling hands in the air.

"That's a good bitch. Now, grab them duffle bags and take 'em out to the car. I gotta debt I gotta pay and it can't wait." Flocka used his gun to motion to Cee Cee to pick up the duffle bags of dead faces. She wiped her dripping eyes with her fingers and sniffled. She then walked over to the duffle bags like she still had a broomstick up her ass and picked them up. She headed toward the backdoor with Flocka holding her at gunpoint.

"You try any slick shit this time, and I'm leavin' yo' ratchet ass in this raggedy ass house, stinkin'," Flocka promised as he disappeared through the backdoor behind Cee Cee.

Chapter Eleven

That night

Cee Cee pulled up inside of the parking lot of The Drunken Monkey. She then looked to Flocka. He was reaching between his legs and grabbing one of the two duffle bags. He then reached underneath the seat and grabbed his gun. After popping out the magazine and checking it, he smacked that bitch back in and cocked the slider on it.

Flocka tucked his banga. "Keep her runnin', I'll be back Asap." he hopped out of the Chevy and tucked his banga in the front of his pants. He then slammed the door shut behind him and grabbed up his duffle bag, heading for the back door of the establishment. He pushed open the door and took a quick look around the dimly lit bar. The patrons were drinking, smoking and/or indulging in a game of pool. Everyone seemed to be minding their own business and enjoying themselves.

Flocka looked over to the bar and spotted the same bartender he'd seen when he and Menace first came in to holla at Raffy. Flocka ambled over to the bar where he ordered up a Heineken and requested to see Raffy. The bartender nodded and walked to the end of the bar, where he snatched a green beer bottle. Turning around, he grabbed a bottle-cap opener and popped the lid on the Heineken. He stopped before Flocka and sat the Heineken in front of him on top of a napkin. Flocka thanked him and dropped a blue face Benjamin Franklin on the bar top.

"That's all you, my boy," Flocka took the beer to the head, throat rolling up and down as he guzzled its contents.

"'Preciate it," the bartender told him as he stuffed the bill inside of his pocket. He then walked over to the telephone, which was hanging on the wall. He pressed a single button and listened to the telephone as it rung. On the third ring, someone picked up his call. He swapped words with whomever it was for a second. He placed his hand over the receiving end of the telephone and looked over his shoulder, addressing Flocka, "My friend, what is your name?"

"Flocka," Flocka called out to him over the loud ass music.

Flocka watched as the bartender gave him his back again and chopped it up with whoever was on the telephone for a second. Right after, he was hanging up the jack and telling him to head up to Raffy's office.

"My man," Flocka tapped his fist against his chest and walked towards his destination. He climbed the staircase and knocked on Raffy's office door. A moment later, he heard a buzzing sound and then the door was clicked unlock. Flocka opened the door and made his way inside of homeboy's office. Once again, he saw Raffy sitting behind his desk, talking to someone over his Blu-tooth. His legs were crossed and he was squeezing a small royal blue ball, looking like he was really into the conversation he was having. Flocka whistled for his attention. Raffy glanced up at him and held up a finger, signaling for him to give him one minute to wrap up the conversation at hand.

"Got cha, thanks again," Raffy disconnected the call and set his sights on Flocka. His eyes then fell down to the duffle bag that the young gangsta was holding at his side. "My friend, is that my money in that bag?"

The Streets Don't Love Nobody

"It sure the fuck is. I threw in interest too, since I'ma lil' late," Flocka walked over to Raffy's desk and dropped the duffle bag in front of him. He then sat down in the chair that was positioned before his desk.

Raffy sat up in his chair and pointed at the duffle bag, saying, "That's my money? Every last red cent of it?" he asked like he couldn't believe the young nigga was dropping a bag on him. He'd already made up his mind to smoke his ass because he felt in his heart that he wasn't going to come up with the money to pay his debt. He had to put his foot in his mouth now though, homeboy had showed up with his due.

"Like I told you the first time, homie, that's you and then some," Flocka stated proudly. "Go ahead and count that shit up, 'cause I ain't leavin' out this bitch, 'til I'm sure we square. I don't want no blowback from this. You Griff me?"

"Right," Raffy took off his Blu-tooth and sat it on his desk top. He then pulled out his calculator and a money counting machine. Next, he pulled the duffle bag closer to him and unzipped it. When he peered inside of the duffle bag, he saw several bankrolls with rubber bands wrapped around them. Raffy licked his lips and rubbed his hands together, greedily. He couldn't wait to run through those bands to see exactly what he was working with.

Flocka sat back in his chair and took the half smoked blunt he had tucked behind his ear. He held it up to Raffy's line of vision, asking if he could smoke in his office. Raffy gave him the nod, and he pulled out his Bic lighter. He stuck the blunt in between his lips and produced a blue flame, firing it up. Flocka sucked on the end of the blunt and blew out smoke into the air. Taking the occasionally pull from the blunt; he watched Raffy count up the money he'd given him.

159

Raffy finished counting up all of the loot and tossed it back into the duffle bag. He then he pulled open his desk's bottom drawer and placed the items he'd use to count the money with inside of it. Next, he removed the portrait from the wall behind his desk, revealing a safe. He did the combination to the safe and opened it. He took out of all of Flocka's jewelry and passed it to him, watching him put the jewels back on. While Flocka was busy putting his jewelry back on, Raffy was stacking the money from duffle bag inside of the safe. Once he shut the door, he laid back in his chair looking at Flocka and grinning. "You know, normally I don't care how I get my money just as long as I get it. But due to these circumstances, I have to ask out of curiosity, how did you manage to get your hands on all of this cash in such a short time?" Raffy inquired as he clipped the tip of a Cuban cigar and pulled out a lighter designed like a jukebox to light it. Holding the flame of his lighter to the tip of his cigar, he sucked on the end of it, and waited for Flocka to answer him

Flocka smirked and said, "I made a few moves, called a couple of markers in. As it turned out, I hadda couple more dollas than I needed once thangs came together."

Raffy blew out a cloud of smoke and sat the jukebox lighter down on his desk top. He knew Flocka was full of shit, but he wasn't going to press his line for the real story. He was just happy to get what was owed to him without having to spill blood. "And there you have it, huh?" A smile spread across his lips.

"And there you have it," Flocka smiled back at him, lifting his hands from off the arm rests of the chair and then dropping them.

There was silence between the two men as they stared at one another. Flocka finally stood to his feet, and decided to break the silence. "Listen, I gotta get goin'. I got some more moves I needa make, so I'll get up witchu whenever. We good?"

Raffy nodded as he sucked on the end of his cigar. He blew out smoke before responding, "Yeah, we're good."

"That's what's up." Flocka outstretched his hand to shake Raffy's hand, but he didn't budge to oblige him. The mothafucka just looked at his hand as if it he'd just pissed and didn't bother to wash it. "Come on, my nigga, don't leave me hangin'."

Still smiling, the Arab shook his head. "I'm sorry, but I'm a germaphobe."

Flocka frowned and dropped his hand at his side. "Whatever, Blood, I'm outta here." he turned around and made a beeline toward the door, his walk slightly off thanks to his fake leg. Raffy frowned when he saw the difference in his walk, but didn't mention it. He contributed it to the real reason behind him being able to pay him his debt.

***

Once Flocka had gotten back outside, he switched seats with Cee Cee and drove her to her house. When he pulled up outside of her house, he put his Chevrolet in *park* and looked at her house, through the windshield. He then set his sights on her. Lightning fast, he drew his gun and pressed it to the side of Cee Cee's head, bending her dome to the side. Fear ceased her eyes and she lifted her hands in the air again. Her eyes were staring out of their corners. Her heart thudded and her palms grew sweaty. At that moment she wondered whether homeboy was going to kill her or not.

"I thought you said you weren't going to kill me," a fearful Cee Cee asked.

"And I'm not, consider this a warnin'," Flocka began. "If you mention anything about how we set up that lick, or where I just dropped that bag off to, yo' ass is done for. I'm pullin' back up to yo' house and I'm knockin' everybody's head off. I don't give a mad ass fuck who up in there. You hear me?"

"Yes, I hear you. I'm not going to say a word to anyone, no matter what," Cee Cee swore teary eyed.

"Good. Now, get the fuck outta my ride!" he took the banga from her temple and sat it on his lap. He watched as she hopped out of his car, slamming the door shut behind her and making hurried steps toward her house. Flocka waited until she was inside before he put his Impala in *drive* and drove off.

Later that night

Levon and LaRon were sitting on the couch playing Madden and sharing a blunt. They blew out smoke from their nose and mouth, as they continued to play the game. The smoke inhabiting the living room made it look like they were inside of a sauna.

"Yeah, nigga, I'm getting all up in that ass!" LaRon talked that shit to his sibling. He was twenty-one points up on his older brother.

"Whatever, mothafucka," Levon waved him off and took a couple more puffs of the bleezy. His face was swollen from Menace pistol whipping him, but it was beginning to go down. "The game just getting started. I still can come back and chip you, fool."

"Bet something, then," LaRon challenged him.

Levon looked at him like he was crazy, twisting his face up. "Bet these nuts!"

Boom!

The door swung open from a powerful force and splinters scattered everywhere. Menace and Fonzell, who were masked up, rushed inside with tranquilizer guns. Their handguns were tucked at the front of their pants. They pointed their tranquilizer guns at Levon and LaRon, just as the twins were grabbing their bangas from off the coffee table. LaRon grabbed his gun first. He whipped around to fire, but Menace shot him in the neck with a dart which was tainted by a sedative.

"Gaaaah!" LaRon winced and dropped his gun. He clutched the dart in his neck and pulled it out. Looking at the dart with blurring vision, he realized he was about to fall asleep. Before he knew it, his eyes rolled into the back of his head and he dropped to his knees. As LaRon fell flat on his face, LaRon pointed his gun at Menace, about to knock his head off.

Bocka! Bocka!Bocka!

Fonzell pushed his son out of the way just in time for the gun bursts to miss him. Pissed off that LaRon had tried to take his son's life, Fonzell dove to the floor and scooted his back up against the couch. He sat his tranquilizer gun aside and whipped out his banga.

"Nigga, you gon' try to murder my boy? I'll kill you, mothafucka!" Fonzell swore angrily.

"Pop, no, I want 'em alive!" Menace called out to his father from where he was inside of the kitchen. He'd crawled there once his old man had shoved him out of the way of the gunfire.

"Fuck this nigga, junior!" Fonzell called back out to his son.

"Alive, pop, alive!" Menace shot back.

"Ain't nobody killing me, both ya'll niggaz dead! That's on everything I love!" Levon swore. He kept his gun pointed as he kneeled down, placing two fingers to LaRon's neck. Having confirmed that his brother had a pulse, Levon picked up his gun. "Neither one of you cocksuckaz are leaving outta this bitch alive!"

Levon looked from left to right, pointing one gun at the end of the couch that Fonzell was taking cover behind, and the other in the direction of the kitchen. He scowled and clenched his jaws, before banging his guns at both locations.

Bocka! Splocka! Splocka! Bocka! Bocka! Splocka! Bocka!

Bullets whizzed through the opposite end of the couch, knocking the stuffing out of it. The other bullets flew through the wall of the kitchen, tearing big ass holes in it.

Fonzell scrunched up his face and turned his head, narrowly missing the slugs coming through his end of the couch. He gripped his gun and clenched his jaws, heatedly. Fonzell was one second from coming from behind the couch and knocking Levon's head off his shoulders.

The Streets Don't Love Nobody

"Junior, you got about ten second before I lay this son of a bitch down, you hear me?" Fonzell called out to his son from where he was taking cover.

"Bitch nigga, you ain't laying shit down, eat slugs!" Levon's face twisted with mortal hatred, and he sent some more heat Fonzell's way.

Splocka! Splocka! Splocka! Splocka!

Bullet's shredded one of the couch's fluffy pillows and knocked more stuffing out of the end that Fonzell was taking cover at.

"You hear me, boy?" Fonzell called out to Menace again.

Meanwhile, Menace searched the cupboards until he found a bag of flour. Crouching back down to the floor, he made his way back over to the end of the kitchen. Poking his head out of the kitchen's doorway, Menace locked eyes with his father and showed him the bag of flour. The young nigga communicated through eye contact the plan he had in mind, and they exchanged nods. Afterwards, Menace disappeared inside of the kitchen, waiting for his time to strike.

Menace counted down to three and sprung to his feet. He called out LaRon's name and launched the bag of flour in his direction. Levon's head snapped in the direction that Menace was at and he fired a shot at him. The bag of flour burst and sent flour everywhere, leaving the surrounding areas cloudy. Some of the flour splattered in Levon's face and temporarily blinded him. Still holding his guns, he bitched and complained, trying to wipe the flour from out of his eyes.

When Menace saw that Levon was distracted, he fired a dart at him. The dart stuck to his chest like a refrigerator magnet, causing him to grunt in pain. Right after, Fonzell came up from where he was taking cover beside the couch and fired a second dart into LaRon's neck. Having been hit with the second dart, Levon fired blindly at Menace and Fonzell. Menace and Fonzell ducked out of the way of the flying bullets. A second later, Levon's arms dropped to his sides and he released his guns. His eyes rolled to their whites and he fell toward the floor, banging his head on the edge of the coffee table.

"Come on, son," Fonzell motioned Menace out of the kitchen with his tranquilizer gun. "Let's get these fucks bound and shipped outta here. I know the cops are on their way, with all of that gunfire, thanks to this piece of shit!" he kicked Levon in the head, slightly lifting it off the carpet. He then tucked the tranquilizer gun at the small of his back and whipped out his gun.

Menace walked into the living room where his father was standing. He sat his tranquilizer gun down on the couch and whipped out a roll of gray duct tape. He went about the task of taping up Levon's and LaRon's wrists while his father held them at gunpoint.

"It's been a minute. I'ma go check on lil' momma," Fonzell told his son.

"I'm good, pop!" Shatira called out.

Menace and Fonzell looked to the staircase. They found a masked up Shatira escorting Delores down the stairs at gunpoint. Delores was bleeding at the side of her head and her hands were held up in the air. She looked like a prisoner of war as she descended the staircase.

The Streets Don't Love Nobody

"Check my boo out, she held it down," Menace smiled and ran over to Shatira. Still holding her gun, she threw her arms around her man's neck and they stared into one another's eyes, kissing lovingly.

"You proud of me, babes?" Shatira asked.

"Hell yeah, you handled yo' business, slim." Menace took Shatira's gun from her and walked over to Delores, clocking her at the back of the head. The older woman hit the carpet out cold, snoring aloud. After passing his lady her gun back, Menace gagged and restrained Delores wrists behind her back.

Menace rose to his feet after restraining Delores and said, "Alright, crew, let's get these mothafuckaz in the trunk of the car."

Police car sirens blared in the distance as the threesome went about the task of loading Delores and the twins into the trunk of the transporting vehicle.

***

Menace pulled up into the woods and killed the engine. He and Shatira hopped out of his car and made their way to the rear of it. Stopping at the back of the car, he pulled out his gun and motioned for Shatira to stand aside. Once she obliged him, he popped the trunk and lifted it up. Inside were the twins, Levon and LaRon, gagged and restrained. Menace pointed his gun at LaRon. The bitch ass nigga squeezed his eyelids shut and bit down on his bottom lip, turning his face for fear of being shot in it.

"Get out! Get cho punk ass outta the trunk!" Menace commanded, but homeboy didn't budge. Angry, he flipped the gun over so that he'd be holding the barrel of it in his hand. He then leaned over inside of the trunk and started whacking LaRon's punk ass upside of the head with it. When he drew his hand back, the handle of his banga was stained burgundy. He took the gun by the handle and pointed it back at his dome piece. "Get out, mothafucka, I'm not gon' tell yo' ass not one mo' time!"

LaRon squeezed his left eye shut so that the blood running from his forehead wouldn't get into it. Using nothing but his legs, he climbed out of the trunk of the car. He missed his step and fell face first into the ground, dirtying his face. As he winced, Menace grabbed him under his arm. "Come on, get cho ass up! Get up on yo' feet!" he pulled him up to his feet and walked him over to where he wanted him to be, forcing him down to his knees at gunpoint. "Stay here! You move, and I'll gun you down, you hear me?" LaRon didn't answer. He bowed his head and his body trembled. Hot teardrops fell from his eyes and splashed on the surface. "I said, 'did you hear me, nigga?'" he pressed the gun to his forehead and lifted his head up, forcing his sorrowful eyes to meet his unforgiving eyes. At that moment, LaRon looked pitiful as fuck. He didn't look anything like the hardcore thug he'd proudly portrayed himself to be.

"Mmmmmhmmmm!" LaRon tried to say something, but the duct tape muffled his voice.

"Youza pussy, Blood, you ain't got no heart, 'less it's somebody weaker than you that chu facing. I don't respect that shit! Matter fact, I don't respect you!" Menace lowered his gun and kicked LaRon in the head, hard as fuck. The mothafucka slammed into the ground, wincing. Then, he slowly pulled himself up from the surface, looking dizzy and shit. "Babe, bring that other bitch ass nigga over here!"

The Streets Don't Love Nobody

Menace motioned for Shatira to bring Levon, the oldest twin, over to him with his gun.

It was a struggle, but Shatira was able to get Levon out of the trunk. He took three steps before his legs gave out on him and he fell to the ground. This was due to his legs falling asleep during the long drive over to the woods. Shatira went to help him up, but Menace calling out to her stalled her.

"Don't help that nigga up, move out the way, baby!" Menace said to her, pointing his gun down at Levon's knees. As soon as Shatira moved out of the way, he fired a shot that sent dirt up into the air. Levon turned his head just in time to miss the bullet; he then got to his feet in a hurry.

Levon forced the duct tape from off his mouth with his tongue and said, "What kinda game you playin', nigga? Huh? If you gon' kill us, then fuckin' kill us!"

"Bitch, shut up and dance!" Menace growled and clapped at Levon's feet, making him dance around as clouds of dirt sprayed up into the air. Once he stopped firing, the oldest twin stood where he was breathing hard, chest jumping up and down. The shooting at his feet left his heart thudding hard. "Hahahahahahahahahaha! And they say gangstaz don't dance." Menace smirked for a second then focused his attention back on Levon's punk ass. "Get cho ass over here witcho bitch made as brotha, Blood, and hurry up!" Levon started making his way over to his brother, but he wasn't moving fast enough for Menace. Angry, the young nigga smacked him across the back of his skull with his gun, dropping him down to one knee. When he tried to get up, the young nigga kicked him in his ass and he crashed to the ground, sliding the side of his face in the dirt. Lying where he was he took a breath, and blew a small dirt cloud into the air. Menace stood behind him, pointing his gun at the back of his

169

head, hostility written across his face. "My nigga, get up and get over there 'fore I split cho wig!"

It took some effort, but Levon got upon his feet. He walked over to where his brother was on his knees and got down on his knees beside him.

Menace stood before the twins looking between them. LaRon was weeping like a little bitch and begging for his life. Levon was mad dogging him and vowing to kill him, as soon as he was given the chance.

"You gon' kill me, huh?" Menace asked Levon with a smirk. He found the oldest twin's threats humorous, given the fact he was in a losing situation.

"You can count on it, mothafucka!" Levon lowered his head and glared up at him. The boy had the look of the devil in his eyes. Having grown tired of his mouth, Menace pressed the tape back down over his lips.

"Pardon me, boo," Shatira tapped Menace on his shoulder and he stepped aside. She stood in full view of the twins clutching a shovel, her hateful eyes staring down at them. "Y'all remember me?" When the twins looked at her like they didn't know who the fuck she was, Shatira pulled the bandana down from the lower half of her face to reveal her identity. The twins appeared to be shocked, then. "Yeah, y'all remember me, so I know you also remember how you were gonna rape my ass that night, right?"

Levon shrugged his shoulders nonchalantly. This pissed Shatira off royally. She cocked back the shovel and swung it at his dome with all her might.

Cliiiiiiing!

The Streets Don't Love Nobody

Levon's head snapped to the right and he fell backwards on his back. Shatira stepped over him and cracked his ass a couple of more times, before she stepped to his younger brother. She kicked him in the head hard as shit, knocking him down on his side. She then hit him in every exposed part of his body, causing him to wince more and more with each blow.

Shatira drew the shovel back over her head in an attempt to strike LaRon's ass again, but bright blinding lights stopped her in her tracks. She and Menace looked up to see who it was approaching, and met the headlights of a Tahoe truck. She lowered the shovel at her side and gazed at it, placing her hand above her brows.

"Relax, babe, that's pop," Menace informed her, watching the Tahoe as it neared them and circled around them.

The Tahoe stopped and Fonzell jumped out, slamming the door shut behind him. He made his way around the back of the SUV and opened the hatch. Reaching inside, he grabbed a gagged and restrained Delores under her arm, pulling her along.

"Now that mommy's here, we got ourselves a family reunion." Menace smiled devilishly.

Menace and Shatira had their backs to the twins, leaving them vulnerable. Making a mental note of this, Levon alerted LaRon and nodded his head to them. Using the sway of his head, he showed LaRon who to attack so they could try to make a run for it. LaRon nodded in agreement of the plan, and they stood up on their bending knees. They exchanged knowing glances, and that's when all hell broke loose.
Levon lowered his head and ran forward, tackling Menace. The collision knocked Menace's gun out of his hand and he

crashed to the ground. Levon then took off running past his brother. By the time Shatira whipped around with the shovel, LaRon was tackling her to the ground. LaRon almost crashed to the ground with her, but he caught himself. He then went to run after his brother but thunder erupted.

Blowl!

The back of LaRon's head exploded and he crashed to the surface. A furious Fonzell, who had kicked Delores to the ground seconds before, walked up on him. He extended his gun at his back and emptied the clip at it.

Blowl! Blowl! Blowl!Blowl! Blowl! Blowl!

Looking up from where she was lying on the ground, Shatira saw Delores running off into the opposite direction. Determined to stop that bitch's escape, Shatira searched the ground for Menace's gun. Locating it, she picked it up and sprung to her feet. Murder danced in her eyes as she chased after her stepmother.

"Tonight's judgment night, bitch!" Shatira snarled, with her gun extended at Delores back as she ran.

Blocka! Blocka!

Delores shoulders danced as she caught hot shit in her back, before crashing to the ground.

Shatira casually walked up on that bitch. She kicked her in the side and demanded she turn over on her back. Slowly, Delores turned over on her back, wincing from her gunshot wounds.

"I guess this is it, huh?" Delores asked as she coughed up blood.

The Streets Don't Love Nobody

"You mothafucking right," Shatira mad dogged her, keeping her gun pointed down at her face.

"Well, here's a little secret I've been carrying, I killed your father." she told her with no remorse. A smile slowly spread across her face, and then she started laughing manically. "Hahahahahahahahahahahaha!"

Delores' laughing agitated Shatira and she emptied her clip in her face.

Blocka! Blocka! Blocka! Blocka! Blocka! Blocka!

"Tell me something I don't know, punk ass hoe!" Shatira lowered her smoking gun and tucked it at the small of her back. She then grabbed a dead Delores by her ankles and drug her back in the direction that she'd come from.

Chapter Twelve

Menace got upon his feet just as the gunfire rang aloud. He looked over his shoulder in the direction that Shatira had ran, and then back at his father, who was blazing at Levon as he fled. At first, he didn't know whose aid he should come to. But after hearing the report of his own gun several more times, he figured Shatira had finished off Delores, and he should go help his father. Having made up his mind, Menace chased down his father. He'd gotten halfway into the woods to find Fonzell trying to reload his gun. Fonzell had tucked his gun under his arm and went to pull out the extra magazine from out of his pocket. Moving too fast, he fucked around and dropped the magazine to the ground. Seeing that Levon was getting away, Menace snatched up his father's magazine and took his gun from him. Fast and expertly, he smacked the magazine into the bottom of the handgun and cocked that shit back. He then chased Levon a short way through the woods, watching him zig zag between trees. Menace pointed his gun and cracked off three shots, missing Levon. Gripping his gun with both hands and aiming it carefully, he pulled the trigger. The bullet ripped through the air. Levon's head snapped to the right and blood sprayed from the side of his dome. He crashed to the ground shortly thereafter. Having seen him go down, Menace tucked his gun and recovered Levon's dead body. He dragged his kill back into the direction that he came from.

***

Menace and Shatira met back up with the dead bodies of Levon and Delores. As soon as their eyes met, they ran towards one another relieved. Colliding, they wrapped themselves in one another's arms and kissing. Holding her at arm's length, Menace looked her over for any wounds and she did the same. Coming to the conclusion that they both were okay, Menace and Shatira looked to Fonzell.

He looked okay, but Menace still wanted to check on his old man. He approached him with his gun extended at its handle's end. His old man took the gun and tucked it on his waistline. He and his son then hugged.

"You good, pop?" Menace asked, general concerned about his father's wellbeing.

"I'm straight, but I could use a pick me up, though." he shamelessly admitted, referring to him needing a shot of dope.

"Well, these mothafuckaz' graves are already dug; me and lil' momma can bury 'em while you get right." Menace told him as he grabbed the other shovel from out of the ground. It had been standing straight up in a pile of dirt, beside a grave.

"Nah," Fonzell shook his head, "I'm not gon' get high in front of yo' girl."

"Pop, she been known that you do what chu do. Ain't no shame in the shit. It is what it is."

"You're right," Fonzell patted his son on the cheek.

Menace knocked on the hatch of the window of the Tahoe and Ducey stuck his head out of the driver's window. "Yo', unc, can you give us a hand?"

"Sho' thing." Ducey hopped out of the truck and followed Menace so they could bury the dead bodies.

Fonzell watched as Ducey, Menace and Shatira attended to the corpses for a while. Afterwards, he climbed

175

back into the front passenger seat and slammed the door shut. Reaching underneath the seat, he pulled out his worn black leather case which had everything in it he needed to cook up dope. Once he had the belt pulled tight around his arm, he administered the shot of heroin. Afterwards, he pulled the syringe out of his vein and removed his belt, sitting it beside him on the seat. His eyes became hooded as the heroin took its effects on him, he found himself nodding on and off. The average person looking at him would have thought he was just dozing off to sleep, but someone from the gutta would be able to tell he was a dope fiend well under the influence. Shortly thereafter, a fog rolled over Fonzell's brain, and he recalled an event from his past once again.

Fonzell sat on his bed Indian Style playing his guitar and freestyling a song off the top of his head. He had an ink pen behind his ear and a notepad lying on the bed before his eyes. While playing the instrument and singing, he'd occasionally stop to write down the lyrics he liked.

Fonzell was crooning lyrics as he played his guitar when he heard a knock at the door. When he glanced at the clock on his nightstand, it was after midnight so he wondered who it could have been at his home at that hour. His curiosity had gotten the best of him so he decided to see exactly who it was at his door. With that in mind, he took the ink pen from behind his ear and leaned his guitar up against the wall. He hopped up out of the bed and made his way down the hallway, making a beeline toward the front door. He peered through the curtains. After identifying who it was on his porch, he unchained and unlocked the door. As soon as he pulled the door open, he was taken aback by the presence of Moochie. Her individual braids hung loosely around her face, but Fonzell could see the black and blue bruising on her cheek.

The Streets Don't Love Nobody

On top of that, she had a busted lip and her right eye was swollen shut.

Seeing tears rolling down Moochie's cheeks, Fonzell took her by the hand and walked her inside of the house. He then stuck his head outside of the door, looking up and down the street for anyone who may have followed her to his home. Once he saw that the coast was clear, Fonzell shut the door and locked it back. He then focused his attention on Moochie, leading her over to the couch and sitting down beside her.

"What happened?" Fonzell asked concerned, sweeping the loose braids from out of her face and tucking them behind her ear.

"He..-he found out about us," Moochie reported, wiping away her tears with her fingers.

"Your husband?" his brows furrowed and his heart thudded.

"Yeah," she nodded.

"Fuck!" he ran his hands down his face, exhaling. He looked stressed as a mothafucka now. Homeboy was familiar with how her husband got down, so he knew he'd be met with his wrath when he found out he was fucking around with his wife. "How'd he find out?"

"I was playing with myself in the bathtub and I called out your name," she admitted. "He busted open the bathroom door, yanked me outta of the tub by my braids and shoved a gun inside of my mouth. He asked me were we fucking around, and if I lied he'd blow the back of my head out." she sniffled and wiped her dripping eyes again.

"Hold on, lemmie get chu something," Fonzell left out of the living room and returned with a few Kleenexes. He sat back down and handed them to Moochie. He rubbed her back soothingly and watched as she blew and wiped her nose. "Go on, finish telling me the story."

"I told him what was up with you and I and he pistol whipped me." she told him. "He pointed his gun at me and was about to shoot me, until I bit him on his ankle. As soon as he went to grab his ankle, I kneed him in the nuts and grabbed some clothes. I didn't even have time to get dressed inside. I heard him coming, so I jumped out of our master bedroom's window. I ran away slipping this dress over my head," she looked down at the flower printed dress and tugged lightly on the fabric. "I hitch hiked a ride to your house, and here I am."

Moochie broke down crying and Fonzell embraced her. He kissed her on the side of her face and rubbed her back, lovingly. She cried her eyes out on his shirt, and he encouraged her to let it all out. Once she'd finished weeping, Fonzell held her at arm's length, looking into her eyes.

"Oh, shit, we've gotta get the fuck outta here?" Fonzell said wide eyed, looking fearful.

"Why? What's the matter?" Moochie asked curiously.

"Nine times outta ten, he's on his way over here. We've gotta get the fuck outta here, asap."

Fonzell hopped up from the couch. He was about to run off when Moochie called after him.

"Yeah?" Fonzell looked over his shoulder, forehead deepening with lines.

The Streets Don't Love Nobody

Moochie looked nervous to tell him what was on her mind as she fidgeted with her fingers. Swallowing the lump of fear in her throat, she looked back up into the man's eyes she truly loved.

"I'm pregnant," she spat it out, watching for his reaction.

"Are you sure?"

She nodded and said, "Yeah. I'm two months. I went to the doctor's appointment two days ago. I would have told you sooner, but that's quite a big bomb to drop on someone."

Fonzell nodded his understanding. He then ran his hand down his face and massaged his chin. "Is it mine?"

Moochie looked Fonzell in his eyes. Right then, he knew exactly who the father of the baby was growing inside of her belly. When she broke down sobbing, he rushed over to her and hugged her, lovingly. He consoled her as she sobbed long and hard, caressing her back.

"Shhhhhhh," Fonzell tried to hush her sobbing, as he continued to caress her back. "Everything is going to be alright. I got us."

Moochie peeled her face up from Fonzell's shirt and looked up at him, tears streaming down her face. "You really mean that?"

"Yeah," Fonzell nodded, looking down at her. "Listen, we've gotta get the hell from outta here. This place is gonna be crawling with old boy's goons any second now."

"Okay. But where are we gonna go?"

"There's a cabin up in the mountains. It belongs to my old man. I haven't been up there in a year, but we should be safe there."

"Alright."

Fonzell kissed Moochie on the forehead. He then packed a few things and grabbed his guitar. Once he came into the living room, he peered out of the curtains to make sure there wasn't anyone outside waiting on them. Once he was sure there wasn't anyone lurking in the shadows to knock him and his girl off, he unlocked the door and headed out to his car.

"Yo', Fonzell! Fonzell!" Ducey called out to his running partner. He was turned around in the driver seat, leaning over into the backseat and shaking Fonzell hard so he could wake his ass up.

Fonzell blinked his eyelids repeatedly, beginning to come out of his dope fiend lean. Once he was coherent, he looked at Ducey to see what the reason behind him calling his name was.

"Yeah, what's up, Ducey?" Fonzell asked with hooded eyes, leaning his head back and scratching underneath his chin.

"Put that shit up, man. It's time for us to roll out." Ducey told him.

Fonzell looked up from where he was in the front seat, and saw the car Menace and Shatira had rolled in before him. His son was looking at him. He had one hand on the steering wheel while his arm hung out of the driver's window.

"You good, pop?" Menace asked concerned.

The Streets Don't Love Nobody

"Yeah, I'm good, son," Fonzell replied as he started storing the items back inside of the black leather case.

"We outta here, OG, I'ma get up witchu later." Menace told his father.

"Okay, junior. I love you." Fonzell told his boy as he pulled open the front passenger door.

"I love you, too." Menace threw up two fingers and drove off.

Right after, Ducey drove away from the woods. Unbeknownst to them, as the red brake lights of their vehicle disappeared into the night, one of the piles of dirt from the graves they'd dug began to move.

***

Flocka stirred woke hearing banging at his apartment door. He searched for his prosthetic leg and found it leaned up against the nightstand. The banging continued at the door as he grabbed it and put it on. He grabbed his gun from underneath his pillow and got up to answer the door, wondering who the fuck it was that had the nerve to disrespect his shit.

Flocka signed once he glanced through the peephole and saw who it was. He didn't know what the mothafuckaz wanted that were on his doorstep, but he sure as hell wasn't up for any bullshit. Flocka unchained and unlocked the door. He then pulled it open, coming face to face with Bumpy's short ass and the goons he'd dropped by the hospital with. They all wore hard faces and looked like they were ready to fuck his ass up.

181

"'Bout time, nigga, you ain't hear my ass knockin' at the doe?" Bumpy spat with attitude. Eyebrows slanted and face scrunched up.

"Man, I was sleep," Flocka frowned up, wiping the scum out of the corner of his eye.

"Well, yo' ass is up now, so throw on somethin' so we can go."

"Go where?" his forehead crinkled.

"To find the dicksuckas that have boss dawg's money. Now, the man gave you twenty-four hours," Bumpy held up his Rolex watch and tapped his finger against the face of it. "I trust you made good on the promise you made, and have a lead on that paypa, 'cause if not, yo' skinny po' black ass is gettin' fitted with cement shoes and tossed over into the gotdamn ocean."

Flocka's eyebrows arched and his nose scrunched up. He clenched his jaws and clutched his banga so tight his knuckles bulge. "Are you threatenin' me while I gotta gun in my hand, mothafucka?"

"Yes, I am, 'cause I know yo' hoe ass ain't got the balls to use it," Bumpy told him confidently. "And even if you do raise that piece of shit nine, the niggaz with me will have already pulled out and dropped yo' bitch ass in this livin' room. Now, like I said, throw on somethin' so we can go find this money." he harped up phlegm and spat on the carpet, keeping his daring eyes on Flocka the entire time.

Flocka was hot as a mothafucka. The vein at his temple throbbed angrily. He was clenching his teeth so hard his head started shaking a little. He'd never had a nigga totally disrespect his gangsta before. No one had ever had the balls to

182

violate him. And even if they did, he would have blown their mothafucking head off. Standing right there before Bumpy and his homeboys, Flocka knew he didn't stand a chance against them. He was outnumbered and outgunned. The only outcome from that confrontation would be him lying in a pool of his own blood.

Coming to the conclusion that the odds were against him, Flocka decided to fallback.

"My nigga, what the fuck you waitin' for? Go! Hurry the fuck up! Come on, come on, come on," Bumpy clapped his hands harder and harder, each time he said 'Come on'. He then pointed toward the master bedroom.

Flocka shut his eyelids briefly and took a deep breath, to calm himself down. Having calmed down some, he headed back into his bedroom to throw on a shirt, vowing to kill Bumpy's punk ass one day.

Two minutes flat, Flocka marched back into the living room, sliding his arms inside of his jacket. As he neared the door, Bumpy tossed a ski-mask to him and he grabbed it. He glanced at it and stuffed it inside of his back pocket. When that little gangsta ass nigga tossed him the mask, he knew they were going to wind up catching a couple of bodies that night.

Flocka left out of his apartment pulling the door closed behind him. As he headed outside along with Bumpy and the goons, he tried to think of a plan that would spare him Big Meat's wrath.

Fuck, this bitch ass nigga Bumpy and his goons are expectin' money and blood tonight. And if a nigga doesn't deliver, then that's gon' be my ass. I gotta think of somethin' quick. I mean, real quick.

"Come on, man, hop yo' ass in," Bumpy said from the front passenger seat. He and the the goons were inside of a van, idling at the curb. Flocka was so wrapped up in his thoughts that he hadn't even noticed that everyone had already gotten into the whip.

Flocka ran over to the van and hopped inside, sliding the door shut behind him. As the driver pulled off, he lay back in the seat, trying to formulate a plan that could get his ass out of hot water.

"Alright, homeboy, what spot we hittin' up first about this bag?" Bumpy looked over his shoulder into the backseat at Flocka. The van they were in had just pulled up to a red stop light.

This shit gon' be foul, but fuck it! I rather it be them than me, Flocka thought to himself. He then gave Bumpy the address of the person he believed had the money from the pickups.

"Cold world! Now, who woulda thought that cho folks had that bag this entire time?" Bumpy shook his head. "I tell you, you can't trust a damn soul these days."

***

Cee Cee was standing at the kitchen sink washing dishes and rinsing them off, sitting them inside of the dish rack once she was done with them. Twenty minutes ago, her parents and little brother had retired to their bedroom, leaving her to clear the table and clean up the kitchen. This was Cee Cee's regular chores and she didn't mind doing them. Hell, she'd become accustomed to them some time ago.

Cee Cee finished the last of the dishes and dried her hands off. She then pulled the drawstrings on the garbage bag, tied them up and pulled the bag from out of the trashcan. Holding the bag at her side, she headed for the front door, singing the lyrics to one of SZA's songs.

Boom!

The front door flew open and splinters shot across the living room. A frightened Cee Cee dropped the garbage bag and backpedaled from the door. Flocka speed walked into the house with Bumpy and the goons on his heels. His face was a mask of anger and the mothafuckaz with him looked like they wouldn't hesitate to pop a nigga.

"Flocka, what's goin' on? Why'd you kick in my-" Cee Cee was cut short once she saw Flocka whipped out his banga. Her eyelids stretched wide open and she gasped. She was about to run, but he popped one in her stomach. Cee Cee howled in agony and grabbed her stomach. She looked at her bloody hands and then back up at Flocka, like she couldn't believe he'd shot her. Right after, she collapsed to the floor, lying there wincing with a mouth full of blood. Seeing Flocka approaching with his smoking gun caused her to fear for her life. She turned over on her stomach and started crawling toward the front door.

"Fuck you think you goin', hoe?" Flocka came around to the front of Cee Cee and mashed his sneaker against her hand. She hollered out as she felt her knuckles being crushed beneath his foot. Flocka pulled her up off the floor by her hair and forced her up against the kitchen counter. "Where's the money, huh? Where's the money you stole from Big Meat?" he asked loud enough for Bumpy and the goons to hear him. He had to put on a show to make it sound and look good.

Cee Cee looked at him bug eyed and confused, saying, "What-what are you talking about? I don't know anything about no…gaaag." She gagged as he wrapped his gloved hand around her neck and applied pressure. She placed her hands on top of his hand trying to get him to loosen his grip, but from the fire in his eyes she knew that he wasn't going to show her any mercy.

"Don't chu lie to me, bitch! I swear 'fore God I'll pop yo' ass. You hear me?" Flocka's hateful eyes bored into hers as he clenched his jaws and caused them to throb.

"You see what chu can get outta that bitch, we'll search the rest of the house," Bumpy told Flocka. He then motioned for the goons to follow him with his gun, marching toward the back of the house.

"Fa sho'," Flocka said as he continued to stare into Cee Cee's terrified eyes. At this time, her eyes had welled up with tears that threatened to run down her cheeks. Their were veins covering her temples and forehead that looked like they were going to explode under the pressure of Flocka's iron-clad grip.

"Why-why are you doing this?" Cee Cee managed to say, trying desperately to pry his fingers from around her throat.

Flocka looked around to make sure that Big Meat's men weren't around. Seeing their shadows cast on the walls from the different rooms that they were inside, he went on to address Cee Cee in a hushed tone, "This shit foul, but a nigga gotta do what he gotta do."

"Bitch, where the fuck is that money at, huh? Where the fuck is that money?" Flocka heard Bumpy barking at whom he assumed was Cee Cee's mother.

"I swear to God I don't know, I don't know about any money!" Cee Cee's mother screamed hysterically.

The Streets Don't Love Nobody

"Please, leave my mommy alone!" Cee Cee's little brother called out angrily.

"Ah, fuck! This lil' fucka bit me!" one of the goons hollered out.

Smack!

A small body fell to the floor after being back handed.

"Fuck it y'all! Ain't no money in this bitch, splash the whole mothafuckin' family!" Bumpy ordered the goons.

Boc! Boc! Boc! Splocka! Splocka! Poc! Poc! Poc! Poc!

Realizing that he had to act now, Flocka released Cee Cee and she hunched over. She held her stomach wound as she coughed, struggling to breath again. While she was doing this, Flocka tucked his banga on his waistline and snatched a butcher's knife from out of the knife block. Having made sure that the other men weren't approaching; he slashed himself across the arm and tossed the bloody knife at Cee Cee's feet.

"Aaaah! You dirty fuckin' bitch!" Flocka's face balled up and he pulled out his gun. As soon as he did, Cee Cee looked up at him with a pair of horrified eyes. She went to plead for her life, but it was already too late.

Blocka! Blocka! Blocka!

Once Cee Cee dropped to the floor dead, Flocka lowered his banga at his side. His shadow loomed over her as he observed his handiwork. He didn't bother looking over his shoulder as he heard four pair of shoes entering the room from behind him. He stood where he was breathing hard from the make believe struggle he'd put up.

"Fuck, man, what happened?" one of the goons asked curiously.

"Bitch, cut me, man, she was 'bouta try to make a run for it so I cut her ass down."

"Damn, G, she got chu good," the other goon grabbed him by his wounded arm and saw the blood sliding down his fist, dripping on the floor. Quickly, he snatched one of the small decoration towels from off the door handle of the stove and tied it around his arm to stop the bleeding.

"Fuck, we ain't gon' neva get Big Meat's money now." the other goon complained.

"Oh, yes, we will." Flocka insured him as he tightened the towel around his arm using his teeth.

"How? Nigga, you done smoked the bitch! Dead hoes don't talk!" Bumpy chimed in.

"I got the name of the nigga that was in on the lick with her. He's the one holdin' the bag. All we gotta do is track this mothafucka down and get it." Flocka informed him.

"Then who? Who has boss dawg's money?" Bumpy asked.

Flocka looked to Bumpy and the goons that ran up in Cee Cee's spot with him. He ran his hand down his face and took a deep breath. He acted like what he knew was stressing him out.

"Come on now, nigga, spit that shit out." Bumpy urged him.

The Streets Don't Love Nobody

Flocka massaged the bridge of his nose and shook his head. Looking back up at Bumpy and the goons, he said, "Menace."

To Be Continued...

The Streets Don't Love Nobody 2

AVAILABLE NOW BY TRANAY ADAMS

The Devil Wears Timbs 1-6

The Streets Don't Love Nobody 1-2

Bury Me A G 1-4

Tyson's Treasure 1-2

Treasure's Pain

A South Central Love Affair

Me And My Hittas 1- 6

The Last Real Nigga Alive 1-3

A Hood Nigga's Blues

Fangeance

Fearless

Fearless 2

The Streets Don't Love Nobody

COMING SOON BY TRANAY ADAMS

Slap Boxing With God

Bloody Knuckles

Billy Bad Ass

www.ingramcontent.com/pod-product-compliance
Lightning Source LLC
Chambersburg PA
CBHW071435100726
47908CB00004B/1161